A Wolf by the Ears

Peter Hildebrandt

For Victor and Joy

Chapter One

"No, you can't take that damned cat with you, Jamie."

"But listen to him. He begs me not to leave him." Gray is making a fuss just like I do. Pa knows that I am, but I go through the motion anyways. I don't push long. Gray's gone quiet.

Maybe he's run off and doesn't want to rub on my ankles anymore, meowing like somebody important needs to care for him. What would he do that for? Do animals tease? I want to ask Pa that, but already know the answers.

"Save your energy, boy," says Pa. "So much with the questions. You be eleven years old now – not six – and you gonna need every ounce you got` before the day is through, just like your mother and your three others after you."

I want to understand though. I, James Hubbard want to know why I have to leave this time. This time I head upriver and I don't want to go, even if I must act like I do. Not that anyone – even Gray – cares what I think.

But even that will happen in its own time. Like much else in this world. Mama says that from time to time, when she's got time to say anything. I'd dozed off a bit. Cat's gone quiet or just gone. Bell sounded out of the darkness awhile back. Bad sign, awhile back.

Now I just hear the chickadees while pulling my pants on and yes – cold enough for shoes this morning. I fish a pair Pa made me out of the corner. They're already too small. I hear voices without as I pull them on – the shoes not the voices; it would be hard to pull voices on. If I don't get out there now, the voices will stop after a time and then I hear a voice I don't want to hear – will not hear because that means a whipping.

I never told you this. I'm not afraid of a whipping. The others are, even Pa is, but I am not. Crazy, you ask? No. Ask that chickadee that sounds close enough to land on my ear. He's not scared of a whipping either.

"You ever had a whipping, Mr. Chickadee?"

"Didn't you hear that bell?" My half-friend Aben asks me, surprising me with a sly grin lingering on his lips.

"No, I didn't hear that bell, Aben." I lie. I heard the bell and Aben knows I heard it. I pull up a plant I know he's gonna make a face for.

"That one ain't ready yet."

"What do I care? You said it yourself yesterday. I'm going upriver."

The dog at the house barks mechanically as if to stop our talk. "Here! Git you in that house and quit from your barking, you'll wake up the Missus' girl again and I don't want to see her looks when that happens."

"Why did you do that, Jamie?"

"I don't care for no dog barking, Aben." I say this before I have returned to the tobacco field.

"We're gonna miss you here," he whispers.

I don't know how to answer Aben. I see him look at my shoes one more time. I know he craves them because Pa makes the best shoes for miles around. I don't want to say anymore about all of this. We've talked and talked about it every day for I cannot say how long.

"They say you be making nails for him."

I shut my eyes and throw down my hoe. The others avert their eyes as if I've got some kind of sick they don't want to have. "Whip me, damn it!" I lean against the chokecherry tree, scrawny little thing and peer up over the bluff to where they're still at it with the tobacco. "I'm going upriver," I shout to no one in particular. "What's it matter if he comes to whip me? I'll never be seeing you again anyway."

Chapter Two

Later, after everyone has melted away and let me be, I sit on a big rock and kick at the drying tan-gray moss. I spy brown moving down among the loose leaves below the rock. The tiny bird cocks its head and takes me in with one bright black eye.

"What are you looking at? You want my shoes too, Master song sparrow? Sure are quiet this morning -- just like the rest of them. Give you the shoes but I think they're too big for your feet and they're too small for Aben's feet or I'd give 'em to him just so he stops looking at them."

"Get back up there to work, Jamie. You won't be here much longer. We need more of those plants pulled before then."

"Yessuh, Master Tim. You don't need to whip me again."

"When did I ever whip you, Jamie?"

Gunshots end the short conversation. Once, twice....three times and from the far end of the field two more shots from the muskets. "What they shooting now?" I ask, more to myself than Master Tim or anyone else.

"You just be glad they fired when they did. Master Tim needed to see what all that is about, Jamie," says Aben.

The smell of gun powder fills our nostrils. Hounds echo down toward the river with their high-pitched cries. Blackbirds exhale from the entire half of the sky in delayed reply to the shots. "Let me come on with you – all of you." I yell up at the sky. "You be flying away from that river. Don't leave me with that river and having to go up it."

"You are lucky, Jamie."

"Lucky?" I want to know what Aben means, I look back at him as I grab as many leaves as I can and stuff them in the burlap sack.

"I hear there be lots to do at Little Mountain, that they be building a big house there."

I am confused. I look up as the blackbirds weave back and forth in their crazed flight. I clap my hands hard, making a loud smack. They shift from the sudden sound like water changing its course.

"No confusion, Aben. Pa says they need nails. I don't want to do that. I want to stay here. At least here I can look like I am busy working."

"What do you know about nails?"

"Nothing. Don't want to know about them." The bell rings me from my thoughts. Too dark now to see the ground anymore or the blackbirds though I hear their annoying clackles and chirps in the tulip trees. Cornbread might be ready; that finally lets me forget all the talk about the nails up at the place called Little Mountain.

Chapter Three

The trip to Massa Jeff's house way up on the hill started for us just after sunrise. The boat we travel in reminds me more of a box that someone might use for packing cargo. Whether boat or box, this thing makes me want Pa. I need Ma. Where is my pa? Why won't anyone explain it to me?

This is nothing but a big smelly box – one with doors on it that can't be opened. Can you tell me why they took Pa from me? No. You just want to sit there looking at your feet. You can't have my shoes no way. Pa made these real nice for me, laid 'em out before he went out to make shoes for the master's children. But I didn't even see him yesterday morning.

Where are you, Pa? What is Ma saying to you right now? I don't care about no nails. I hope Creola told you – remembered to tell you that my old shoes I left there by the door are for Aben.

"Rocks ahead!" I hear the shouts from outside the barred window slots. "Pole left – now right; don't hit them rocks. Got valuable cargo for Master Jefferson here."

"Valuable cargo?" Someone asks the question from down along the bench. "Is that cargo gonna save his nail-making operations? Don't know about you folks, but I needed to laugh."

Laughs hack and chop at the air before a thump fills this space. No more talk after that. Poling pushes this barge in jerks too slow for me to care about. Pa would smile at all that right now and make a sign to show how silly it all is, how silly they all are.

"Nails are hard work. Did that for a time and had

to quit. You master that though, you get on his good side, Master's good side." The man does not look up. I see from his face it took all he had inside of him just to say that.

"I don't know nothing about nails." I want any talk to end and I think this will do it.

"You will, after you get there." A boy with a gash on his left cheek speaks. He looks at me until I can't stand looking at him anymore.

Outside a dog's high-pitch bark punches the air from the riverbank. Someone claps and shouts far up the hill and all sounds cease except for the growing thunder of rough water over the rocks along the river banks and the piping of sparrows from the unseen briars. I see nothing in the gloom of this big wood box, not even their eyes anymore. Someone wheezes when they breathe. Where are you, Pa?

Chapter Four

Our pitiful wagon is not moving near as fast as all the rest of them. That other wagon has cotton on it. I can see the fuzzy haze leaking out of the sides – and the thing is piled up with iron tools the full length of the other side, I'm thinking that may be in order to hold down the cotton. Something. But even that old thing beats us out.

"What are you staring at? It's just a cotton wagon." Some big boy of about 19 stares at me as I look.

"I just see nothing along this road goes slower than   we   do."

"There's something that goes slower. Damned box

turtle."

The wagon breaks into a wave of laughter that disintegrates into knowing murmurs.

"Just the way it is," continues the older boy. "Least today. Tobacco's up for now. Brush is cleared off and not ready for the wheat to be planted yet. He's not in any rush to have us eating any of that cornbread up there or the scraps of ham what may be left until there's work, clear work to do."

"Don't believe anything you hear about any ham or cornbread from Massa Jeff," whispers one small woman, hair tied up into a tight ball on the top of her head, and a person I'd not even noticed until just now when she spoke. "Old Jeff likes to tell his friends us slaves cost us so much in food. Truth be told none of us could live on the mealy old dried fish he doles out like we be chickens rushing for food. He buys for himself the food, eggs, tomatoes, sweet potatoes and the like that the slaves grow themselves in their own tiny gardens rather than starve on his worthless dusty old fish."

A pair of men, hair graying at the top of their heads mumble agreement and nod their heads.

I hear the sound of hooves moving at a clip before I see anything. Another series of wagons block my view of the rider. He breaks through the knot of wagon traffic, heading directly for us.

"Surprised, Boy?" The young man sees my mouth fall open before I close it when he holds my gaze.

"You'll need to put some speed on this rig. He's wanting them straight way." The man is black, in cotton clothes with fine collar and a perfect ruffle down the front of his shirt.

"Ain't you ever seen a free black man before?"

"Free man?" He rides off faster than my mind can find words for another question.

"He rides off almost as fast as that there killdeer," says the young man.

"Killdeer? What sort of name is that?" Never heard such as that.

"What do you call it then?"

"I always thought they was killie-birds; it's what I always heard them called." I feel silly now.

"That's a new one on me."

"Me too," echoes a white-haired man in the corner of the wagon.

"If he's never heard that name before, that is something," blurts the first man. The wagon erupts into laughter.

I feel as if I want to sink into my linen shirt head and all just like a box turtle and snap my old flap shut to make the world go on without me. "I'll be free like that some day, same as that man. Then I will go back and see Pa."

They don't laugh this time. What I have said darkens their faces some way. I want them to explain how my words have angered them somehow.

"First off, quit saying you don't know nothing about nails," says the first man.

"Get it in their heads you don't know nothing about them and they get it in their heads and you be back out with the tobacco, or the wheat – or flax seed," says the white-haired man. "Nails is bad. I ain't lying. But Massa Jeff loves his nails. He be down checking on 'em most the days. Could he wave on them magic sticks – wands – like some conjurer, that's where he'd be first to make his wishes happen, to find someone for that part of the business."

A soft breeze plays with the back of my neck. I bring air into my nose real slow. This lets me think for a time about what White Hair's just said. Killie birds – sorry, killdeers – sound like they are going to attack us if we get any closer to their corner of this road. Can roads have corners? I won't say. Sure they're gonna find something funny in me saying that.

Master Mocker Bird makes his nasty sounds, kind of like someone's twisting a stick through a tight knot hole. Then he flashes his white flaps and tail before reaching the top of a hawthorn tree. What's this? Boy, why you crying now? I want the tears to stop. Can't get that song out of my head, the one Mama always hummed and Pa'd sing in harmony just under his voice while they worked. "Yankee Doodle come to town, riding on his pony.....sticks a feather in his cap and calls it macaroni...."

"You just keep it up, Mr. Yankee Doodle," says the first man, chuckling. "You be Mr. Nail Boy soon enough."

Chapter Five

You're up bright and early this morning, Mr. Wren with your tea kettle – tea kettle – tea kettles over and over again. I can hear you. But you don't want me seeing you, for sure. Wished I could make lots of noise without anyone seeing me.

"What you doing up so early?" The younger man who has no name, at least one he's told me yet leans back on his elbows and stares at me. Straw covers a big part of the tattered blankets he shares with the white-haired man.

"Couldn't sleep," I say soft enough that he squints to hear me.

"Well, that's what I see; you ain't sleeping, Boy," he pauses. "It's noisy in here with these snores. They know, or their bodies know that nobody's asking them – no telling them – to work, they gonna do the opposite of work. We traveling so everything's a bit different. Them drivers probably had too much Rattle-Skull last night; they're not in any hurry to get moving this morning."

A rooster crows as if to point out that still, everybody needs to get up.

"I'm gonna be like that man we saw yesterday – the one on horseback what flew right by us." I quick-like feel bad for saying as much.

"Not something you have a say in, boy."

"I'll run away if they don't let me work for my freedom."

"You hush. You say that. But come here." He reaches over to the white-haired man and lifts his shirt as he sleeps. The old man's back is a mass of tiny ridges that look like the mountains 'round here would look like if I could I fly way up like a wren. "He never once tried to escape, but still, anyone takes a notion to, a beating a whipping can come – sure as rain, just don't always know when the next rain's coming."

"I ain't afraid of that." I lie. But part of me doesn't lie either.

Chapter Six

This is for me. Me? What's that mean? Snoring's long stopped. The dream with Pa and Mama, me holding the wood handle while he tries to stick the shovel back, but it just doesn't work, comes again, goes on and on.

Mama's there asking me a question, but I can't really hear what she's saying. Some kind of dream like that one or that one always awakens me.

In the blackness I sit hearing the snores once again, those of the others here on our trip up to the big place called Little Mountain, Monti-cello; words from another language Pa said. I say snores, all's quiet now and I miss their snores, miss even that hard annoying sound. At least it's a sound. Outside I hear the peeps from the frogs and the owl trying to scare me with his whoooo-alls. And in the distance I hear the whippoorwills calling out like it is the end of the world tonight.

I remember Mama's tears. They come easy and I don't feel this pain in my chest like I do right now. But then I think about what makes the pain thump in my beating heart. Pa's eyes look good one minute like he's gonna be strong for me and come to see me when he can – just like he says. And then I see those eyes fill up like there's a spring just at the back of them and now I am crying but don't want to be.

Owl's tired of all this. Gone on to the place owls go when they's sleeping. I do hear some crazy mocker bird singing down in the brush somewheres. Eyes still wet. A Mocker bird stabs at the air with his nasty bird shout like he's telling me to get on his back and sleep. This isn't your time he's screeching.

But this is my time. When no one's awake to tell me otherwise. This is my time.

Don't forget that, James. You may not have much, boy. You don't even have your Mama, Pa and little sister any more......but you've got this right now. I'm up and prowling like old Gray my cat, walking this trail I take the risk of someone finding me out. Gray's got Mr. Owl to watch out for. I take my own chances and say no words to anyone.

Chapter Seven

Three days later I am up again, nail straight in my straw. Been raining the past few days. But I think of all the time gone by without my morning walks and my heart hurts because I feel more lost in some ways than I am lost to Pa, Mama and Gray.

Doors chained shut from without. Good. Means maybe no man sleeps outside, musket cradled in his fat lap. Keep on snoring, Sir. This may make a sound or two. I move along the wall swift-like feeling each of them slots of the shed. They are all slapped together on this messy thing. First few are not loose in the least. No amount of shimmying will let them give.

"Suppose you ought to be getting up and moving," calls one voice.

"Suppose. Ain't in no hurry today. Put a pot of coffee on that fire and I will be," says the man right outside. I see him lean back again. He ain't in no hurry just like he says.

I am about to give up. Then I tug on one board that looks solid but in reality is all spongy. It gives when I pull and falls right from the nail holes.

Not much right around here. At least I can see the sun starting to rise. I work my way down to the creek and drink. Freedom. This is what it feels like?

Dogs bark just off from the creek as if to answer me direct-like.

"What you think you're doing, boy?"

I'm about to say I got lost and something about hearing a cat sounding stuck in a tree. But his hand across my face becomes the only thought in my head – more than anything else.

"What's your name, boy?" He finally speaks after dragging me back and throwing me in with the others.

I act like I've not heard him. A willow switch across my neck makes me suck in a breath.

"Mass Jeff don't whip his boys they say. But you ain't up at Massa's yet. Name?"

"James Hubbard, only I go by Jamie, like Pa does – "

"That's too important a name for you, I reckon."

"Pa gave it to me," I whisper as much as hiss. I look up in his tired eyes until he turns away to look at the horses and the wagons the others have already started shuffling towards. I want to say I'm gonna carry that name – the one thing I have been given – for as long as I breath. I'm backing up, backing up my eyes waiting for his to look my way once more. But he takes more note of his dog going off after some squirrel that has fallen from a branch than what I just did to him. I smile to myself somehow. I look around at the others waiting for their glares but they never come.

"You better put spring to your step, Boy," says the younger man who helps the older, whip-scarred man to a place in the wagon. "They's gonna be more'n that welt on your neck from that man's switch if you don't move and quit your getting away. You can't be doing that no more."

I want to say to him that I didn't get the switch. But I can't say any more. I just keep smiling to myself. I touch the tender place on my neck. When I do the switch's lash comes back. But I don't even feel it so much. I just feel something else. I told him about my name and he said no more. He didn't hit me nor say I was wrong. I am James, James Hubbard and no one will be saying my name is too important for the likes of me. "Look! A bluebird."

"Never mind about no bluebird," calls the young man once more from his place beside the old man.

But I pay him no mind. I pick the poor creature up by his tail; he's still fresh – no ants crawling out of his eyes – and I put him on a fence post I saw where they nest. This feels right. The feathers seem even bluer. At his neck tufts of orange ruffle out. "You got a name too, Mr. Bluebird, just as important as mine."

"Just get you up here in the wagon! Tell Massa Jeff all about your damned bird – and see what he says."

"When I'm done making him his nails, I will."

The wagon jerks into motion like a mule being what a mule is, all stubborn-like.

"You won't ever be done making nails," intones the old man.

Chapter Eight

The wood seat hurts me where I sit. I look over at the old man and think that he must have it even worse.

I've been crying for my mama and pa and Gray and even my sister, tears that have no end it seems. No one pays any mind to tears. They've seen them before and will see them again.

"This time I swear I'll be good enough to work on the building of the new house." These words come from a man I heard called Jonah, but one I never really heard a word from before.

"Don't always get what we want," old man says. That seems to stop the talk. But mumbling at the far end of the wagon keeps on like the wheels themselves. Rain starts up again and I try to keep warm under the coverings.

At last the sun's back out. I don't feel any warmer though. I think of all I've heard so far and nothing sticks in my head, all a jumble of talk, telling me what I have to do, what I can't do, where I'll go – never why I have to go there. Just I that I have to, impressing on my mind.

The wagons stop while the horses get watered. Slaves up front – slaves – their word and I hate it, head down to the creek with wooden buckets to get water. I hear the waxy birds. Mama says the Missus calls them waxwings. Look nothing like wax to me as they flutter over my head. They twitter as a group and fly to the berry bushes down near us.

Back and forth, up and down over and over – they can't make up their minds. They don't have any freedom. They are slaves to those red berries they can't get enough of. A blue jay calls them over to the other side. "He's their master and he's laughing at them."

"What you talking on, boy – James. You say the craziest things," the younger man says. He stares at me and then looks away from the frenzied waxwing birds.

Chapter Nine

"Where's my pa?" It is the first thing I say as I'm waking up. Now that I look and smell where I've been sleeping, I wish I was sleeping still.

"You're a mad little boy. Your pa's long gone from here – never was here." The young man says the words and nobody has time for them it seems or they choose to ignore the hurt in them.

"I dreamed my pa grabbed me around the shoulders real tight just like he used to trying to get me to howl but he never could." I don't care what they all thinks and I see from their eyes they somehow feel something for themselves too – maybe from something way back in their own minds.

"Don't you start in to crying again." The old man says the words quietly. "Don't matter no how, now that this rain's leaking in through the canvas covering. None take note as your face be long wet for sure, anyway."

"I'm not crying. Pa's gonna come. Wouldn't have felt him so strong and his arms round me if it weren't so."

Wind blows the canvas flap up, spraying heavy rain on us as if to verify what I just said. The mules shudder for a long moment before plodding on. A wren calls out his tea kettles. Sounds loud enough that it's in our wagon and from the other side the red bird stabs the air with his call as if to keep us from talking or even thinking.

"There must be something 'bout you to make him cart you all the ways up to make nails," whispers the young man after a long while.

"Aha. He knows that pa you always going on

about. Good man. Mass Jeff's hoping some of that's rubbed off on you, little James," adds the white-haired man.

"I just want to be home with Pa. Don't know anything about that – or making nails."

Chapter Ten

I miss everyone paying any attention to me. Rain's let up and now it's just cold. They threw some horse blankets – that's what the old man called them – over us. They're scratchy and they smell like piss. But when you get over all that they still get you warm.

"I'd like to have them shoes of yours, Boy," the young man says, finally talking to me. But it's not really me he cares about but Pa's shoes, shoes he made for me.

"My pa made them for me."

"You ain't gonna have no pa doing stuff like that for you where you're going."

"Leave the boy alone." The white-haired man says this even without looking at me, with his eyes mostly closed.

No one talks for a time and the wagon creaks along not seeming to be going anywhere at times.

White-haired man's slumped over and snores. The young man's eyes are closed. His face squints up so I can tell that if he's anything like me he's hungry. Others have nodded off and lean up against each other.

"I don't want to be making no nails." The words slip out before I can stop them, thought going to my throat, tongue and lips; nothing to stop it. I wait. The wind whips the canvas up on my face and blows up underneath the pee-soaked blanket. Right now I crave someone to say something. Say I've said it too many times already. Tell me I am a fool, stupid, not a person to be around – just say something. With all these nameless people, quiet-like I feel sad, dead. "Say anything, something." Wind gives me her answer. Smells like cow manure.

Chapter Eleven

Pa isn't coming. The thought punches me in my gut. Don't matter how good these eggs, hoe cakes, corn bread and coffee are, I still wrestle to get that thought in my head.

"Your pa ain't coming so quit going on 'bout him." Young man said that just enough to me that no matter how bright the sun shines in the morning or how nice the breeze rising up from the creek may be I'm punched down with the words. I have to keep my head clear but all's a fog.

"Pa's coming up here." I shout it as I get up from the table.

"Keep saying it, Boy. That surely makes it so," says the young man, who yesterday I heard the old man call Clay while someone else calls the old man, Eustus.

"Don't have to listen to you if I don't want."

"Kind of hard when we can't get no further from each other than a few feet," says Clay.

I decide not to say anything at all to him or anyone else and walk outside the barn where they've been giving us food for the past few days and look all around.

"You ain't gonna head down to the creek are you, James?" A white man says the words, words that cause me to look directly into his eyes.

"Suppose not. How'd you know my name?"

"You suppose not? I knew your name before you even arrived here. Your reputation precedes you." The man is already moving out of earshot. He has a bunch of sheets in a leather book under his arm. I don't think much more of him for a bit.

"Massa Jeff done took your mind off your pa." Eustus has already started moving bushels of grain from the long row on the ground up into the line of wagons.

"Massa?"

"Don't usually get to see the man."

"What be a reputation?"

"I ain't sure what that means. But if that man says something about it to you, I'd be finding out just what it does mean."

I pull up one of the bushels and hand it to a young man on the back of the wagon. I go to grab another and my foot catches on a root. I fall, knocking over the wheat bushel. "Guess a reputation couldn't be this; never done this before."

"Boy, you better keep it so. Massa sell you back down the river. Something tells me he's a patient man. But everyone has their limit."

Chapter Twelve

Lots of robin red breasts up and down in the trees here. They sure sound happy. The robins don't act like they are cold or anything. I just have come out from that shed for a time. Can't stand the smoke. Not used to that and it's dark in there – too dark for me.

"Never mind 'bout those birds, James. I be trying to show you how to do the nails. That's what you are here for." Samuel is a patient man, patient as one man can be I suppose. Others line the sides of the old shed with their fires working on their nails.

"My name's not James. I go by Jamie, just like my Pa."

"Well I ain't heard nothing 'bout that, Boy – Jamie, if you please. Sure you didn't come upon the idea to make you Jamie and not James as Massa's records man tells me?"

"Wish Pa was here to explain." I get back to my stool and pull on the tattered gloves once more and start hammering.

"Ain't doing you any good to hammer till you get it hot. Ain't gonna get any hotter till you get the forge blowing on these coals. Be good if your Pa was here to remind you. You ain't hearing a word I say to you."

This last makes me sit up on my stool and take note. I hear the tightness in his voice. I decide not to say anymore – just as Pa can't say anymore to me.

I see the papers in the white man's hands when they come in to check on me and what my - my output, output is the word – might be. I dream the page holds words from Pa, something that the man would read to me or I could read for myself. I asked Pa once about reading the words on the page. He said I couldn't ever do that 'cause no one would ever teach me to. They do, the law says, they go to jail.

The idea splashes over me like water from one of these wooden buckets here beside the fire, in case we burn ourselves. Expensive property does have to be taken care of.

"I hate burns!" One of the boys yells the words reacting to something he just did. None look up though we all feel bad for him. I use my legs to express my empathy in letting the boy be alone. Pushing the worthless door open I walk over to the charcoal oven to fill it with more wood fuel. I understand now what they were talking about with the charcoal. Creating charcoal, that smokey endless job is as much a part of the nail-making work as the nail-making itself.

Chapter Thirteen

"Ain't fair Pa can't write me and even more than that, I can't write to him." I don't know that anyone hears my words as we walk out of the shed at day's end.

A creaking wagon pulls up the hill full of stuff from Poplar Forest Plantation. I know some things have been made by Pa, crates of his handmade shoes. I dream of some letter from him in one of those crates.

"These be from your pa." Samuel hears what I said and starts pulling off the crates of materials, some are surely shoes Pa made. "What madness." A crate on the bottom sounds alive. Samuel pulls off the lid with the flat end of a hammer and Gray scrambles up out of the top.

"That's my cat, Gray."

"He don't act like he's your cat or anyone else's."

He'll be back, I want to say. I got water in my eyes now. "Pa writes to me with stronger things than ink or words."

"Maybe your Ma be doing the 'writing'."

I let it be. She wouldn't take the time.

"Cat can't be staying around in here." Jonah sounds tired.

"I burned me again. Won't be doing no nails no more." The boy over in the corner throws down his hammer and starts to cry. A man crosses the shed and takes the boy by the arm and heads for the door.

Funny thing is, outside I hear the switch on his back but I'm not hearing anymore crying. Burn must have hurt more than the whipping.

"See this," Jonah picks up a mass of the metal. "You don't worry about this stuff."

"You mean that part what's like tree branches?" I ask.

"Right. You want to call it that then take this part what's the trunk and get them hot and hammer it out." Jonah backs away as the man that I heard some call Randolph stops at me. "You're worse than any of the others, boy. Look at that mess on the ground – waste. No hope for you. You be best out with the tobacco and wheat."

Jonah puts up his hand and scoops one of my latest nails from up off the ground and hands it to him.

"Gonna take a lot more than this one for him to avoid getting sold down the river."

At those words the boy who has just been

whipped starts to whimper once more. When he catches the man's eyes he forces himself to stop crying and starts to hammer in a frenzy. The man starts toward the boy once again.

"Jamie here just started, Sir, and for just that short piece of time he's got some skill, promise."

"I thought his name was James."

"I go by Jamie, just like my Pa – "

"He ain't used to how things are done around here with manners, either," whispers Jonah.

The man stares in my eyes a long moment. I cannot tell what he means to do, whip me or say something else. "Guess there must be some who be worst in nail production. If there must be a worst it ought to be the newest one here. But Master Jefferson is most concerned about output and we need more nails than this in a hurry."

Gray pushes the shed door open and encircles my ankles. No one seems to know what to say. The purring for all its quiet, drowns out enough sound that the chickens down along the lower pastures can be heard.

"Somebody's shirt's on fire. I smell burning linen or cotton; that cat's gonna have some burnt fur as well. Get it out of here." The man is gone with those words.

I grab Gray and toss his purring body out into the drizzle. "Pa, you do love me and you have not forgotten me." I say the words out loud to calm me as much as to get me to not think about the whimpering boy or the looks on the faces of those other boys.

"I smell a skunk," whispers one boy.

"I do, too," another chimes in.

"I like that smell," I add.

"You're crazy," shouts the first one and most start

laughing. They quickly begin chattering and pushing away from their work tables. Not long before some sounds outside and then hard footsteps heading in this direction get them back to their work.

"Here! Not like that," a boy I'd never noticed before grabs my tongs from me, turns over the die and helps me to position the nail just right before the top tamps it perfectly into place. "You be new for just a bit." He turns back to his own work and gives me a sideways glance as I do the next nail better. Then he nods his head to show me I got it right. He has the biggest pile of finished nails beside him on a small wooden pallet. "Look, in case you didn't notice yet. Here is the best way to make a nail." His voice is just above a whisper but tense with a sense of its own importance. "First you heat the nailrod in the fire in the forge. Then, it be best to hammer one end to a point on an anvil before sizing the length of the nail – see how he does it over there? Watch him. Next stick the pointed end of the nailrod into the header. Break off the excess metal. Shape the head with four to eight blows of the hammer."

When I have a moment I glance from work table to work table. The boys who talk the most, laugh and wander around have the smallest piles of finished nails in front of them.

"Ain't gonna do you no good to work harder," says a boy who surely caught me glancing at the piles.

"Just hush, Jacob," says the boy who just helped me. "And I forgot to tell you this. Each type of nail made requires a particular heading tool. Particular be one big word. If it's too large for you, think special."

"You can get him thinking it makes a difference, Ben, if he makes a bigger pile every day. I ain't gonna lie to the boy."

The boy he just called Jacob looks up at me and

shakes his head as if to get me to ignore him.

"Well tell him to just ask Tom about it."

"Don't be bringing up Master Tom."

"That boy ain't my master."

The door squeaking open cuts off further talk. "You boys ain't producing; you be talking," says the overseer they all call Gabriel Lilly. Behind him stands a lanky boy who looks like he needs to be in here helping us out. The lanky boy shakes his head and smiles. The others turn to their work to avoid dealing with him

"Is this James?" the lanky boy asks.

"This be James," says Lilly. "He likes to be called Jamie."

"Hello, Jamie. I'm Tom."

I want to ask him why he doesn't have a work table, but I hold my tongue and am glad of it. Pa always said if you are unsure of whether you should ask a question, it is better to wait a bit. But then he is just a little bit, too.

"You never see me working in here, Jamie. I got other things to do. Father calls them pressing matters when he needs to go. I got pressing matters without."

Silence meets my questioning eyes. Pa's right. They present me with some questions needing answers. Not my place to ask them. Mr. skunk must be close again as his smell crowds out my questions. The boy next to me, Ben, throws another nail on the pile and smiles. I close my eyes and imagine that smile being Pa's.

"Even when I'm big enough I won't be working in here," continues Tom. "Even when I be seven years old next year, Papa says I don't need to worry. We are all one family, one big family like a Roman family. Roman families had slaves. But there are things about the slaves that are different."

"I don't think Roman slaves made nails," I offer.

"Just don't get into it with him, boy, and Master Tom, you run and find your pa. I think I heard him calling – "

"My Pa's in Philadelphia, silly – "

"Well then, your ma or sister." Jonah helps the boy move toward the door and shuts it firmly – as firmly as the rickety thing can be shut.

The clinking of the nails and shattering of the wasted parts continues. I'm not gonna be the one to break the silence. Young Tom chatters for awhile outside. Then he makes an announcement, in a voice loud enough to be certain that we hear it inside the shed. "Nothing can stop the man with the right mental attitude from achieving his goal. That is what Pa tells me to be true."

"Can a slave have a goal?" Jonah's question is met with laughter.

Then Tom is crying, something about falling on his knee. Any sound of him is gone as quick as it came – at once.

Chapter Fourteen

A red bird hops around in a puddle from all the rain of late. The color red stands as almost a separate taste in my eyes. It makes me feel sad about where I need to go this morning. I notch my little chokecherry to start another day. I lost count of the number of notches already climbing up the scrawny trunk.

"Why do you mark that tree every day?"

"I don't know, Jacob. I just do." I want to tell him it's one thing I can do because no one told me I can't do it.

"You need not to make so many nails each day now. Just makes us look bad. Not like it matters. I heard someone tell that Massa Jeff had wrote down in his journal that you be the biggest waster of the the nailrod. Don't think that be so no more."

My pile has already grown compared to the others a few hours after Jacob told me not to be so fast.

I see him glance to the table where each of us leaves our piles of nail work.

Laughing comes from the other end of the work shed. A table falls over.

"What's going on in here?"

"Jamie came and knocked my table over!"

The man looks my way. I just shake my head. "Doesn't look like Jamie here has time for that with that pile he has.

In the distance the sounds of hammers and the shouts of men directing each other seem to announce the clear need for the nails we are making – or trying to make.

"I'm bored!"

"So am I – "

"Tell it to Master Thomas. He'll be back later today to check all these piles. He needs a barrel or two more nails than these." With the flat-ended wood scoop he clears all the piles into one big bucket.

"There goes your big pile, Jamie," says Jacob. "No one can tell whether you made more than us or not now."

"He knows," I say as the man shuts the door behind him, leaving us with all the smoke inside.

"Don't mean he's gonna tell anyone, though."

I wait for the red bird to sing his what-cheers, wait some more. Silence. Guess I'll wait as long as it takes for anyone to note that my nail piles are always bigger than the others each day nowadays.

Chapter Fifteen

"Watch out, Jamie." George is always ready to warn you. We are outside and not doing our work for once. George is too little to take part in most games. I'm backing up, backing up, backing up, backing up my pa taught me good when it comes to games and I don't look back. I haven't heard anyone one. I'll be fine. "I'll be good, little George." Just as the words come out of my mouth I feel the side of Jonah's chest as he squats on all fours and I splay across his back and the onto the ground, legs and arms no where to go.

"My turn!" yells George. The others all laugh at his sudden boldness.

I start the round all over again. "Tulip, pansy, poppy, daisy, clover....." with each word he has to back up three strides while everyone makes the sounds of grasshoppers on a summer's day so low that George doesn't think there's anyone behind.

But Jonah's a master of sneaking up and keeping people thinking he doesn't get in the way.

"Petunia!" I shout.

George takes one and a half steps back. Mid back up with clearly no idea Jonah's sneaked up behind him he topples and lands firmly on his head or neck; hard to tell in the tall grass.

Whoosh. Snap. "What the hell do you all think you are doing?" Smith brings a switch across Jonah's neck and face. Jonah dives in the tall grass covering his face and screaming.

"We's told to go out yonder until the – " The switch hits my mouth and teeth. On the next stroke I catch it and rip it from his hand. Before I can think, a slap knocks me onto my back. From the corner of my eyes I see Jonah pull me across the space between the booted leg and my ribs.

"Enough." The voice is soft yet firm-like to stop Smith in mid-kick.

"They're out here away from their work and needed to be reined in." Smith speaks before he can think to hold his tongue.

"Were they permitted any time away? Why don't we ask them?"

"Yes, Master Jeff, we was not told we couldn't stop to frolic in and around – "

"Were not told, Jonah."

"Yes, Master Jeff."

"Lying bastard," hisses Smith.

"Smith, may I speak with you?"

"Papa, Papa!" Young Tom dangles a newly caught frog by a green-brown leg. "Will it bite me if I don't let him down?"

The boys can barely contain their chuckles and confusion flusters both men for a long moment. Neither seem to know what to do or say next.

"Whatever has been happening, you must pause and think about what has transpired each day. Yesterday there were 597 – the most nails in one day ever. Had you a clue of that?" Massa Jeff takes the switch from Smith's hand and smacks his own thigh, wincing slightly.

"Frog got away anyhow, Papa. Can't bite me now."

Chapter Sixteen

Mockingbird doesn't make any sense this morning. Singing so pretty out there, just the other side of the shutters when such ugliness lingers in here like an old white woman talking all sweetness and then turning on you in a flood of lies. Wet wood smokes things up real thick while those new boys at the far end aren't caring no more for their nails than anyone else is.

"Thought you said you hate this work." Jonah reads my mind with his words. I do hate those cussed nails but I see what the others have at the main house under construction with these nails.

"I want me some better clothes and – "

"No, Jamie, don't work that way." He scoops up the growing pile by my table and bench. "You make more, they got more reason to keep you right here."

"And I ain't wanting more than that and to someday – "

"I know your next words." Jonah raises a hand and I can hardly keep my words inside me.

"But..."

"Meeeeeeeeeow."

"But nothing. That old cat of yours is having some problems."

Gray's going no where when I reach him. Tom has him by the tail and laughter trickles from his mouth like a creek overflowing its banks after nights of rain. "Old Mr. Gray's not fond of having his tail pulled, Tom."

"Cats like it when I do this. Look! He's smiling, Jamie." I pull his iron grip down the length of Gray's tail until the hold loosens enough for Gray to break free. "Haaa!"

"See. He ain't happy to have it pulled, Tom. That's why he bolted away."

Tom's face gets all flat and sad. He looks like those new boys who just started at the other end of the shed – wanting something else to do in a hurry.

"Let's get him back." Tom heads in the direction of a grove of trees where Gray fled.

"Don't think that's a good idea, Tom." But he's taken off and I chase him knowing Smith's gonna want to beat me if I don't get inside. Tom falls into a ditch just at the edge of the woods. My heart races as I reach him. There's a cut on his face now and the fall's knocked the breath out of him.

"Jamie? Boy you get in here!" Smith shouts the words but I can tell he doesn't see where I've gone off to.

"Boy, you got me into a fix, for sure."

"My name's not boy. My name is Tom. Your name is Boy."

"No, I got a name. That be Jamie." I hear the steps before I see who they belong to.

"There you are, Tom. You need to let Jamie get back to his work. Hello, Jamie." Massa Jeff pulls Tom up out of the ditch from where I've been struggling with him. I smell fruit – berries and grapes on Massa Jeff's breath – a good sweet smell what makes me think of summer and Pa and all the rest in my family.

"Jamie here has the record so far for nail production," Massa Jeff opens the page as if to show me something, then closes it remembering Virginia's laws about teaching me reading and ciphering, I suppose. "He's retrieving my boy, Smith."

Smith stands on the other side of the ditch, hands on hips. I scramble up out of the mud, brushing off the leaves, twigs and wet sand.

"Jamie's in our family, right, Papa?" asks Tom as they walk off in their own world.

"Of course, son."

"Just the same as ancient Roman families like you told me, ones including the slaves in the family, Papa?"

"Just as I told you, Tom."

Chapter Seventeen

I just can say that the air has that sweet happy smell it can get when something's about to happen with the sky and clouds. Rain's coming. I make my water out behind the sweet gum tree once more, reach to a nearby puddle formed after last night's rain, one beside the old poplar and scoop me a few drinks of water to replace the liquid I just let out of my body.

"Jamie, get your sorry little black hands in here." Smith has a bucket of nails already in his hands. I can tell he ain't yelling. He's just saying this 'cause he got his nails already this morning. He looks at me then looks away. Can't bring yourself to say it, Smith can you? Who did the most of those nails for you? I hold my tongue.

"I hear Massa Jeff has a privy being built right inside his house, heard little Tom talking on it and

using my nails to – " Build it, I want to remind Smith. One. Two. Three. Four. Four always does it.

"You just keep your thoughts inside that simple head of yours, Jamie. And no, ain't your nails."

I want to say my head is just as good at thinking as yours, Smith, but I shut the sorry shed door behind me with a hard thump. The thought that pops into my mind next is something what I can't keep from my mind. That is that Smith, the only thing that makes you better than me is the law, which says a man or woman goes to jail if they teaches me to read or write – be they black or white I suppose.

"Hello, Jamie."

"Hello, Tom. Tom, your father teach you to read?"

"Of course. He teaches me whenever I ask him to."

"And when was the last time you asked him to?"

"Today."

He goes to writing on the loose dirt floor with the scraps from an iron rail leavings. He looks up when done and smiles.

"Spell anything?"

"You should know. You got one and I pulled his tail for good luck today."

I cringe at the thought and squint down at the cramped letters. The clinking of the hammers on iron rods continues all around me. None seem aware of this law being broken right in their midst. Massa Jeff be the most important man in the whole country I hear and his slave boy squats, writing C - A – T down in the dirt at our feet.

"Don't matter none." Tom kicks the word away with his foot. "Gonna find Gray and tie a switch to his tail, Jamie."

"You leave old Gray be."

"How you gonna stop me?"

I don't want to go back to that damned shed. Not right now. Rain's finally stopped. Gray's following me around the woods above the creek and I got me a big fat piece of cornbread still warm with some butter dripped on top to sit with here on the bank and eat.

"Gray, you ain't no dog. Git back with them other cats." The hammering from the shed sounds out from the place even though I can't see it from here. Cuckoo bird eyes me from the bare dogwoods. "I be just like you Mr. Red-eyed cuckoo. Don't need to say a word if I don't need to and yes, Gray you go ahead and run off after that sparrow way over there. Be the cat, not no dog."

No one's out here with the cold, though I heard Massa Jeff say spring's coming in three weeks. Oh no. Here he comes.

"They been looking all over for you, Jamie."

"What of it, Tom?"

"They's counting the nails now. Papa's watching—"

"Counting along with them no doubt."

The cuckoo calls. I hear him, but suddenly, like Tom's papa I don't see him now but I know what he's doing. Glad Tom's interested, too. He wanders off in search of the bird. "You get a whipping, Jamie if you don't have enough nails."

"Thought you maybe was lost, Tom, and no. They counted my pile and your papa found I got double the number of anyone else's pile."

"What's double?"

I grab Tom by the wrist and pull him up. "Never mind. We got to be back."

"Tom!"

"Over here, Massa Jeff," I call back to him.

Smith pulls out his switch and smacks it on his trouser let. "Can't be going off again and expect to avoid it, Jamie."

"Papa, what does double mean? Jamie says he has double the nails in his pile."

I catch Smith's face out of the corner of my eye without letting him see me directly. His face reddens somehow.

"Double means twice the amount of something present," says Massa Jeff hardly loud enough for himself to hear the sound, let alone young Tom. "Jamie here doesn't have double the amount of nails in any of the others' piles; he has triple the amount."

"What does triple mean? Smith gonna whip him harder for that?"

A rust-tailed hawk screams ragged and lonely in the windy sky. "Better watch out, Gray. You may catch that sparrow. You don't be careful, Master hawk catches   you."

"They always gonna be able to catch you, Jamie, when you run off?" asks Tom.

"Need to warm you by the fire inside, Tom. You're shivering, child." Massa Jeff sweeps Tom up far above the ground and sets him on his shoulders. Everyone seems to forget everything said. Mr. Hawk screams two more times and drifts beyond the barren tulip tree limbs. He floats off – free – bored with this talk, too; and

Gray lives to witness another day, I suppose.

Chapter Eighteen

"Tom, sometimes I don't feel like being the maker of the most nails." The smoke, the bellows, the fresh pile of nail rods – fresh from Philadelphia – and the endless hammering hammers the spirit right out of me.

"Papa knows you're the best, Jamie. He writes your nail numbers down each day in his book."

"Well that's real nice, Tom." But even today the little boy's words watchful and wise as they are don't free me from my worries one bit. "Of course I need me some pan bread right now – something to fill this hole in my gut, too." I take the shiv and sharpen the end of a nail, cut it off, slip it into the little hole and hammer down the head. Another one. Just like all the others but still one all alone. I sneeze and it feels good, clears all the dust from my head.

"The rest of them are outside wrestling now, Jamie. Why don't you go out?" asks Tom.

"Got to get my bucket filled up – "

"But you just said you don't always got to be the biggest nail maker."

"Changed my mind. Now you git out and play 'round with them others."

"Don't want to. Doing something else."

Gone at last, not so bad when everyone's gone. Don't have to look at anyone or answer their questions. I don't feel so bored because I'm not watching them be bored. "Damn!" Burned myself. Haven't done that in a while. About had it now.

"Where you think you're going, Jamie?" asks Smith at the shed door.

"Going for a walk by the creek."

"No. Others been rolling around outside, cutting up. Guess you missed your chance."

"Thanks I get for keeping that bucket there full."

"What was that?"

I don't answer. He's not hearing any more words out of me for a while. Smith says I can't go outside after I've been doing all this work already. Don't need to waste my breath on him anymore.

"For being the one what Massa Jeff inks onto the pages as his top nail maker you ain't too good at making the best of your time now, are you, Jamie?"

Clink. Clink. Clink! I fan the flames after hammering. The horse whinnies outside and I know that sound better than any of them and the bang of the flap on the wagon as it's unloading. More nail rod's arrived from a place Tom likes to say as much as he can get the word out of his mouth. Philly Dell Fia. That horse, his whinny, that wagon and the iron load it carries chains me to this place more than anything Smith can ever do or say. "Well, where you been, Master Tom? Others quit their wrestling and trying to work a long while back."

"I didn't go to wrestling, Jamie. You said you was hungry. Here's pan bread, still warm and some fresh milk from Papa's store."

Chapter Nineteen

"Papa says being higher up's better for the health." Tom pulls at my hand. Don't get up there that much. Never had any interest in seeing this. Boom – Boom - Boom.

"Putting a new roof on the new building there, Tom?"

Tom breaks loose from my hand and runs across the wide grassy place. "He's the one what made most those nails you are using!"

I run across and catch up to Tom. "Don't think they heard you, Tom. All that noise.

"We heard him." Boom. Boom. Boom!

Underground. What are they digging up underground for and taking those wheelbarrows of dirt away from there for?

"Come on up here, Jamie!" Tom climbs to the top of a fresh hill that's recently been created.

"Hey, quit that, boy. Stop throwing dirt at me."

"Jamie, you gotta catch – " Tom falls over at the other side of the mound. His voice cuts out as his whole body falls smack into the soft earth.

"Boy, you got this dirt in my hair, eyes – serves you right." I don't really mean it. Tom's just a little one. When I reach him he lies sprawled, head down lower than his legs and arms. "Tom, boy, you all right?" I look around to see if anyone else sees this scene before them. My heart's jumping out of my chest. "Tom?"

"I vex you, don't I?"

"Don't know what that means but get the rest of the way up."

"Papa says that means to trouble someone very greatly."

We walk the length of the trench that's been dug and watch the men digging the new section while others most certainly don't need to be smoothing that floor to the trench already smooth from the feet of countless people walking up and back in a constant stream. "What's that smoke down at that end for – where I smell bacon frying?" I ask the question not thinking Tom would have an answer for me.

"That's the kitchen, silly. Don't you know anything, Jamie? They be making food – well, one or two slave cooks - for both all the slaves and the free white visitors and Papa up in the house. There will be fancy dish recipes from France, Spain, Italy and Germany cooked there, too. None of those foods for the slaves, of course."

I don't answer him. Don't want somebody younger than me acting such a way towards me.

"Papa says he don't – no doesn't – want no, sorry any, smokey old kitchen near to his house when it's all done. This will be all covered up after a time. When food's done it goes from there to the inside of the house. People don't even have to bring it up stairs from there, it will be what the dumbwaiter's for."

"Makes no sense to me – vexes me."

Tom grabs some dirt and throws it on my head. I put my foot out and trip him.

"The other Jamie, Jamie Hemings, vexes Papa. Never wants to be at the nail shed."

I want to explain the truth about the other Jamie but hold my words inside. Tom doesn't see things as I do, as the others do. This doesn't stop me from fearing for the other Jamie. Smith is bad enough; this new

Smith named Gabriel Lilly is 100 times worse.

"Gonna help me up or you just gonna stand there? I smell fried pork, what Papa promised tonight."

"Sorry, Tom. Sometimes a boy just can't get his mind moving enough to get his body to do anything." I pull Tom up from the soft dirt.

"Here!"

I sprawl backwards onto the pile, hitting my head on a rock. "What did you need to go and do that for?"

"Now you can wait for me to help you up – a long, long while, Jamie." Tom is off. I manage to struggle up to my elbows and then to my feet and watch him scramble down the long trench all are working on. He looks back as if to tell me to run after him. Then he sees some boys his age to wrestle with. Had enough of Tom.

Chapter Twenty

"They's talk of you having your own place, boy." Smith mumbles the words and I don't look up from my cutting and hammering.

"I'm not knowing what you be talking about, Smith," I offer, finally. In between hammer strikes, mine and all the others, I hear Mr. Mockingbird singing to save his life, sounds like. I like the song of the bluebird better, nice silent warble – almost like a giddy whisper sometimes. Must not impress Mr. Mocker; never have heard a Mockingbird sing the quiet song of a Bluebird – not flashy enough for him, I suppose. Bluebird is nearly like me, not wanting to get in anybody's way but wanting to let all know he's around – sky on his back –

"Did you hear what I just said, boy?"

"You said I'll have my own place--"

"After that."

Bang. Bang. Bang! "I'll tell it then. He told me that you be moving, Jamie, because you got the most in your pile each day. Then there only be one Jamie in here." That is the most I've ever heard that other Jamie speak. He is a Hemings – cousin somehow of Tom. With the Hemings all's a bit different. "I'll take over as the top nail maker once Jamie Hubbard is gone."

Everyone has a good laugh with that one – even Smith. But when I look up next, Smith is no where to be seen. Lilly sits in the corner looking at his ledger book, one like Massa Jeff has but he holds it wrong side up so I can tell he's not really looking at it as much as he's looking at us. I hold his gaze, throwing another nail on the pile.

His face reddens when he sees the book is top side down. "That ain't enough from you boys back there."

"Jamie's a Hemings. He don't need to fret over how many he's made," says Dan.

"That so? We'll see about that."

"Talk to Smith 'bout it," I offer. I make three more nails in quick time. Too much for Lilly. Right then I know our mistake. He is out the door, not gone for long enough as far as any of us is concerned.

Chapter Twenty-One

Here is a much better place, up here on the side of the hill, for breathing than down along Mulberry Row.

That is the name they've all taken to calling the place where the smoke, dust and stink from everyone's sweating bodies explodes at times – just like ole Lilly's likely to explode. I can tell it's gonna happen. Just don't want to be in that shed when it does.

The red bird pounds the air with his cheeps, defying the breeze. Only reason I'm up here is heavy rains must have held back that order of nail rod Massa Jeff is wanting us to use.

Bang. Bang. Bang. Hammer blows always in threes onto the nail heads mixed with Mr. Red Bird's chirps. Now I smell potatoes frying with onions and I am missing Mulberry Row.

Monty – Chello, Tom says that is what his papa names that place up there, for little mountain in a foreign talk. I call it foggy hill. Most of the time it's wrapped in thick fog. What's it matter what I think?

"Jamie?"

"What are you wanting, Tom?"

"Just looking for you. Wondering what you are doing up here."

"Getting away from the likes of you."

"They've been looking for you. Nail rod's been in a time."

"What?"

"Hey – wait for me, Jamie."

I've gotta watch out for that low spot. Come running down this slope in a hurry and it catches me every time.

"Ohhhhh." Tom found it just the same.

He is quiet when I reach him. I kneel down and help him up thinking he hit his head on a rock. He's smiling when I turn him over.

"Can we do that again?"

I shake my head and motion to the bottom of the hill, the nail shed far down the end of the row. Tom makes me pull his full dead weight to his feet, pretending to be a dead boy. "Get up. Just get yourself up."

Tom laughs and finally starts walking trying to catch up to me. "You afraid of a whipping, Jamie?"

"No."

"Then why do you always make the most nails of anyone?"

I stop and stare back at Tom. His question is a good one. I take a deep breath, sucking in the smells of potatoes and bacon and onions frying below, somewhere on Mulberry Row. "They gonna give me my very own place for nail-making soon. I make even more and they give me some nice things to wear. No more holes or snips." I put my finger through the hole in my shirt on my chest and stick another down my trousers to let my finger show there.

"You think in time you'll buy your freedom, don't you, Jamie?"

Not sure how to answer this. "That would be nice."

"Papa never allows such a thing as that to happen."

Now my voice has no air behind it. Feel like Gray trapped in that crate Papa sent him in, the one Tom still catches that poor cat in at times.

"Other Jamie, Jamie Hemings, talks of his freedom from time to time – 'specially when Lilly nags him."

"Lilly takes that kinda talk real personal, Smith never paid it no mind and they was still more nails came out of Jamie Hemings with Smith overseeing."

Hammering has already started. The nail rods form a small pile on the table. Lilly doesn't seem to see me when I walk in and sits. Got other business on his mind.

Chapter Twenty-Two

A new fresh day rises with the morning. What shall fill this time directly ahead? Mr. Wren stands on the fence post as I head to my new place, a shed of my own. The space is just the right size for me. Smith must have got the fire going already.

"You like the fire I started for you?"

"Where you come from, boy?"

"Who you calling 'boy', boy?"

"Tom." We both start laughing at our silly words. "Thank you, Tom. I thought Smith started that fire for me."

"Smith? Now you sound like you been in your own shed too long – Smith. He must be leaving you alone because he never does such as that."

We spend the next little while picking up leavings from the wood splitting done a while back. Wood's dry enough and splintery. I throw more on Tom's sad effort at a fire and go outside for more wood.

Mr. Wren bursts from the brush with his singing only now I can't see his pretty mask. "You be smart to stay hidden, bird. Old Gray would love to spike you with his claws quicker than I can finish one of them pesky nails."

"Bang. Bang. Bang." I finish the head and pop the nail out. "Clink." The small sound of the metal on the pile in the box only makes me realize how much more work I have to do to finish up, to fill that box.

"What you worried about, Jamie? You act like you're never making enough and – "

"Tom, go out and get more nail rods in the main shed." I didn't want to hear his chatter anymore.

"Bang. Bang – "

"Jamie, get out here!" Tom motions with his chin. The look in his eyes makes me shudder. The door on the nail shed swings crazily. I see the boys running from the shed. One, two at once, then three, then one stumbling out.

"A fire, Tom?" That is all I can manage as we run all the way to the shed. Tom's handful of nail rods loosen and he drops some as we go. We're both too anxious and worrying and rushing to pick up the precious iron material. What would Massa Jeff say? How'd he write this in his journal books?

Screams come from one side the shed, where I used to have my work place. Look inside and there are just boys backed against the shed wall while over in the corner a body lies slumped onto his side. Lilly's still beating the form, still whipping taking breaths every so often, then checking himself after a pause as if to gather up fire wood for the flames burning inside of him.

The rest quit from their staring and take a cue from me being there to silently get themselves out. Four minutes. Four minutes. Something tells me that Jamie Hemings – the one who owns that body on the dirt floor, aside from the other that own it, Massa Jeff – isn't gonna live much longer unless I do

something in the next four minutes, maybe four

seconds. Tom tells me a second is officially much shorter than a minute, a minute much shorter than an hour and so forth.

"Jamie, do something for t' other Jamie before he dies." Tom's words get my own mind sharpened again.

"Lilly, you need to stop now. Ain't no life in this poor boy." I hear myself say the words above the sounds of the leather strap. My gut churns with everything that can be down in that part of my body. Something in me feels about to bring on some puking but I can't even control it. "You be wrong, Lilly. Now just stop!" I yank the strap from out of his hands as there's sweat all over those hands. "Whatever you think this boy's done or didn't do, chances are he didn't do it. You already broken him. Need to let him be now. He be lucky if he survives this beating what you – " I didn't see that coming I think and there are flashes before my eyes for some time. I push up from the ground after the blow. Opening my eyes I see Tom sneak off with Lilly's strap. Lilly catches this out the corner of his eye and lights out after Tom.

"Jamie, you be all right now." I lie. His body feels like there's no air to it, without life when I lift it up and carry it from the stinking nail shed. Fires be burning still. Some of them fires dying out. Jamie's fire burns bright and I nearly cry looking at that while the one that owns the fire lies in my arms. "Best go back inside. Get them fires going again. Work gets your mind off this."

"We ain't of a mood – "

"You want to be beaten like poor Jamie?" Another of them asks of the first boy, Joey.

As I head for the cabin Jamie stays at, there is no more sound from outside the nail shed. "I want there to be some sound from you now, Jamie. Please answer me. Are you any kind of alive?" I feel a slight tightening of his hand on my wrist. Then there is water at my eyes.

Chapter Twenty-Three

"Jamie has trouble with holding his head up, Tom."

"Did he say why, Jamie?"

"I'm just sitting here when I can waiting for him to say something. Even be if it's one sentence for one day's time. That would be good – "

"How do you know what a sentence is? You ain't supposed to know that."

I don't want to speak with Tom right now. He reminds me of that mocker bird outside, chirping this song of that bird, then some other bird then the red bird; can't ever settle on just one for more than a minute before the next starts up.

"Woooo!" Jamie makes a sound that ceases my running mind and Tom's open talking lips what never stop. Then Jamie rolls over to the other side of the pallet bed facing the gap-filled wall where he gets sick. Not sure how this can be as he's not had much to eat, near as I can tell.

"Can you move more than your arms, Jamie?"

"Not sure he can even hear us, Tom--"

"I hear you, heard everything you've been saying for days," whispers Jamie.

Tom brings him a fresh cup of water he holds up to Jamie's lips until he coughs just after drinking a gulp. "When you going back to the shed, Jamie?"

"Look like I'm ready to go back to the shed?" The

question proves too exhausting for him and his head falls back on his pillow.

I think of the pillows Tom showed me up on the hill in Massa Jeff's rooms and this is no kind of pillow such as that, more like some cast off clothes not even fit to be slave-worn, tied all together into a lump that –

"Jamie? Tom asked you a question."

"Must not have heard it."

"Tom stands right here, not sure how you couldn't have heard it. Asked if you got more nails to make."

"I made my pail for the day. Now I do those that you could have done had Lilly not – "

"Don't say it, Jamie."

I stop the talk and pick up a nail that some how has ended up here on the dirt floor of this shack, not even fit to be called a lowly cabin. Outside the slot-like window I see the buildings taking shape up on the hill and hold a nail in my vision. They can't build one of them without nails and lots of my nails.

"You gotta get some food in you, get your strength back, Jamie.

Jamie turns with all the strength he can muster. He shakes his head slowly. "Ain't going back in there."

"You got to, Jamie." Tom suddenly has a perplexed look on his face.

I know what Jamie is saying. He ain't going back in the nail shed. To not do that means two things and I don't think getting beaten to death is the one thing to be choosing.

Chapter Twenty-Four

Gut feels a bit stormy this morning. It's a sparrow kind of day, making just a bit of sound but lying real low too, just like a sparrow stays in the dead blackberry brambles.

Yesterday old Gray bit Tom. Gray's not himself, either. Something going on out there with some pretty white cat that makes Gray not taking to Tom's singing. Out of the blue he just goes and bites Tom's ankle. Tom isn't even talking about it anymore. He's all taken with this telly-scope he borrowed from his pa. Speak of the devil; Tom that is.

"Here, Jamie – look in this end and watch what happens."

"I don't need to be looking into something when the doing's gonna be something to give me a whipping."

The other Jamie doesn't hear my words above the clanging in the shed.

"You just look into this side and your hand looks to be a mile away."

"All right. Yes. That looks to be so." The tube is smooth and cool, even with Tom handling it. I turn it to the other side and right away don't like what this telly-scope does. Lilly is walking down Mulberry Row heading in this direction. Gray is gone. He doesn't like Lilly either. "You best be putting that back on your pa's three-legged stand, Tom."

"I will when I'm all done."

I can't argue with him right now. Lilly fills the doorway presently and I let my eyes shift over to Jamie who pretends not to see Lilly.

"When you going over to your own nail shed, Jamie? It's all ready for you and set up."

"Not now, Tom." Tom notes the tension in my voice. Finally he shifts himself to one leg, standing there to test his balance as he likes to do at times. He catches my eyes and I nod in forced encouragement just to break the hold of the lingering cloud lingering in our midst.

"Not enough once again." The blow knocks Jamie to the ground. Clanging stops and the others rush from out of the shed as if a skunk has appeared in the other doorway.

"Quit, Lilly. Beat your whip on my back instead."

"You making plenty, boy. Why would I beat your back?"

"So is Jamie here....real fine since you – "

"I'm gonna tell Pa 'bout this, Lilly. He don't even ever want whippings. Calls them necessary evil for them other folks with slaves, but not for him."

Tom's words change everything in the space. Lilly stops for what feels like might be just a quick spell, but doesn't have the heart now to do more than pull his whip up to coil it. Tom with no hesitating takes his pa's telly-scope and stabs Lilly in the gut. Time feels suspended from the shed rafters for a long while.

"Gotta bring Pa back his telescope," adds Tom. "He will be needing it to survey the new building going on up at the top of the little mountain."

Chapter Twenty-Five

"Massa Jeff says you got all day today to get ready, get to feeling better, Jamie."

Jamie closes his eyes and gives me just the faintest of nods before he lets his eyes flicker back open. I don't know exactly how to read them. Jamie is a Hemings, like Tom, some kind of cousin but far enough from Massa Jeff to be catching stuff from Lilly if damned Lilly takes a shine to do as such. But since he carries the Hemings name, Jamie feels he deserves better than that.

"Everybody thinks I'm a feared of Lilly." The words take the breath out from me and I have to suck some in all of a sudden. Jamie motions with his chin to the drinking gourd hanging on the peg by the door.

"Be right back with a gourd full for you, Jamie."

"Get back here!" One of the overseers is trying to break one of his hounds of wandering off. He talks nice-like to the dog mostly. Dog doesn't know any better and in its head sees the error of its ways as Tom puts it.

I fill the gourd at the well. Fires have started up. I smell some cornbread cooling on a rack outside one shed. I grab some for Jamie and me. Then I think of how the Massa's overseers treat us worse than their dogs. We've got a lot more in our heads and can play one person off another and plan; no hound can do that, well, maybe not as easily as us.. Gray's found my ankles just before I reach Jamie's shack and nearly trips me as he blocks my steps all purring and fussing. "Sorry I took so – "

"Thanks, Jamie. This is real nice. You have some, too."

"Just a bite. You need it more than me."

"You be fine, then and surprise them all and be back first in the morning." I can tell I said the wrong thing. Jamie doesn't answer for a long time.

"I still got them real good shoes your Pa made for you, and what you gave to me."

"What do you mean?"

"Just saying I like them and I'll never forget you for giving them to me – I feel my moving feet in style and comfort now, and remember how you made me feel, Jamie. Nobody remembers what it is people say or even do. Nothing of those words that matter. You do remember how somebody makes you feel, though."

Chapter Twenty-Six

"Jamie's not in his shack, Lilly." The finality of the words makes us feel jubilant, justified – scared to death for poor Jamie all at the same time. Lilly is radish red now.

"What you say, boy?"

"My name is Tom, Tom Hemings." The words are barely out of his lips when Lilly shoves Tom up against the planks of the shed.

"You tell Massa Jeff I did that to you and tell him, too, one of his slaves be gone." The door slams shut behind Lilly.

I pull Tom up and brush the dirt off his knees.

"I will tell Pa. I don't think Lilly thinks I will but I ain't scared of Lilly – not like Jamie was."

Gray cares nothing about any of this talk. He's

looking for me for some reason. His sorry meows tell me he wants to tell me something or other. The hammerings and clippings and bellows for the fires in the main nail shed go on. "Go start my fire for my shed, Tom. Could you do that for me?"

"While you sit and let Gray purr and rub all over you?"

Gray must know we're talking about him. He gets himself up on my shoulders. I'm not gonna get me much work done like this, for sure. I hear Tom breaking the small sticks for starting the fire and smell the smoke of the early flames. It drifts my way ever so shyly.

"Look over by the stump," Tom calls from inside the shed.

"What are you talking of, Tom?"

"You'll see what I'm talking about."

I toss Gray up into the air to get him moving. He lands in a pile of leaves just one side of the stump Tom speaks to me of. It is the tree – what's left of the tree – I once helped chop down when they searched for a place for my own nail shed.

"See it?" Tom has the fire going well now. I hear the heavy breath of the flames eating up the wood chunks, some from this very tree, now just a stump.

"Not yet, I don't – " My eye catches the bundle resting calm-like just starting to get covered by dirt, sticks and leaves.

"See it now, Jamie?"

"Yes." I pick up the wayward bundle and finger the rods already starting to orange over with rust. In my mind I see the boy, just a little boy barely more than nine that mysteriously died one morning. Jamie knew what happened to that boy's skull when he mislaid these nails. That's why Jamie couldn't stand to work anymore, made him sick in heart, sick in head. Now he's gone and I fret even more for him in some ways, some ways not.

"Do you like the fire I made for you?"

"Thank you, Tom."

"What did you do with that bundle, Jamie?"

"Guess."

"You set it free?"

I nod slowly. With all my might I threw that offending bundle that caused death to one little boy for his losing it and who knows what for an escaped boy involved with it as well, far into the woods.

"Like you said the other day, Jamie, you got things good over here. You make the nails you can. Pa and the others get you good things, place closer to mine – "

"My freedom?"

"You wasn't forced to do any of this to get your own place. Jamie be back; he be OK."

So much I want to say. It doesn't matter how good I got at making nails. I am no different than an anvil, bellows, clipper, tongs, looper, hammer or anything else you want to say. "Easy for you, Tom. Your Pa owns all this. He does well by you."

"Does well by all them others."

"Hog shit!" I feel bad I said the words. I like Tom. Some things I don't think he'll ever understand though. "Tom, just think 'bout when we used to catch lightning bugs in a jar. They be shining like all get out when we catch them and jar 'em. But what happens not too long after lidding 'em in there and owning them like we got our own six-legged slaves?"

"They quit their shining."

"But we take that lid off and let them out and they start right back in to their green-yellow glow once more."

Chapter Twenty-Seven

"What are you doing back in here, Jamie?"

"I can be about this place when I want to, Tom."

"I know. But why would you want to be?" Tom's question is left dangling like a spider web that has been ripped apart in a doorway by somebody walking through it.

It is cold and wet outside. I made all the nails, my amount, my quota Smith used to call it, before Lilly came here. I am walking about, picking up loose nail rods making sure Lilly sees me doing this – chopping firewood, bringing in shirts off the rope where they're hanging to dry all the while avoiding the work of settling matters with the two new boys, Sam and Jonathan. "The new boys be scared of Lilly."

"After what he done to Jamie Hemings I don't blame –"

"No. They do not need to be scared."

"What do you mean, Jamie?"

Clank. Clank. Clank! I hit the nail extra hard to give it a real sharp end and to keep the boys we've been talking about from looking our way. "I need to visit the privy."

"But Jamie, you just –"

"Come on and just shut your mouth."

"Alright, Jamie."

We slowly cross Mulberry Row and head down the narrow, well-worn trail to the tiny wooden shack. Someone else makes his way back on our way, passing us midway down the path. Before they pass I find a nice smooth rock from among the leaves to give the impression I am truly about my business at the privy. I feel like there must be something I can do to control the things that aren't feeling quite right today in the shed. I look over to my shed and see that Tom's got my own fire going over there for some reason. But it can burn out for all I care.

Speck of gray-brown shoots up from the brush. This surprises us both for a moment. Sun plays on the wet early spring twigs, cold with days of rain. Both Tom and I see the jagged head of the tit bird struggling with a long green worm he must have found down in that rotted stump. He wants to scold us awhile with his low and high chirps and then call out his peters from up amid the higher branches of the dogwood tree.

"Thought you had to use the privy, Jamie."

"You know I did not get to use it a short while back." We draw close enough to the shack that everyone avoids. But now stand farther enough away that we do not smell the privy.

"What do you want to tell me, Jamie?"

"I be worried about those two new boys."

"What for?"

I study Tom's gray-brown eyes. He does not seem to see things my way at times and at others he sees things different – better than I do. White-throat sparrow calls his lonesome Sam Peabody song a few times making me lonely for Pa and home. It passes. "Them boys is frightened is all, Tom."

"What do you mean?"

"They is scared of a whipping from Lilly. See what he done to Jamie and at all costs want to avoid that. I know too, they've lost a bundle of nail rod."

"Which one?"

"Don't matter which. They just needs to fess up. They both admit they don't know what happened to it. I don't believe Lilly will even take the time to whip them. He will get over it. Lilly knows Massa Jeff needs nails – bad – not time wasted on whippings and I –"

"Jamie. Listen."

Shouts, no screams come from up the way. We start in to running up the muddy pathway. My heart starts to racing, not from the running but from where I sees the noise coming from. Boys circle all around something struggling on the muddy ground just outside the doorway. Blood oozes from the faces of both boys. Looks like Lilly's just got there, same as us.

But though they're still grappling on the ground, one of the boys, Brown, I think, isn't really doing much. I see other boys holding the one they call Cary back though Brown looks to be fairly lifeless now.

"What you gonna do to him now, Cary? Them boys really need to be holding you back?" My question puts them all at ease, even Tom who does not look able to stay at one place more than a moment or two.

"I can't be putting up with it no more!" Cary blurts the words between breaths. "I be looking for that missing bundle of nail rod most part of yesterday, lost sleep worrying 'bout it and looked all this morning – I ain't wanting one of Lilly's thrashings again. But turns out he had put my bundle under his own box lid the whole time and he be acting all sad-hearted to me, making me feel like he be pulling for me wondering where that missing pile could be." Cary can no longer hold to his words. He looks down at Brown Colbert on the ground, blood oozing from his head where his hammer blow cracked his skull and his eyes appear to be off at some other place none of us know.

"I got Massa Randolph." Tom can barely get the words out. I had not even noticed his going off. Soon Randolph has two of the bigger boys carry Brown to a nearby shack.

Does not matter whose shack it is apparently. They're fighting for this boy's life and nothing else matters. For one piece of a shining moment, sun searing through the gloomiest of clouds on a dark day, I am thinking that they want him living because he is a human being just like them and not a chunk of nail-making equipment for making Massa Jeff money for Monticello groceries, but that moment passes as do all other moments.

Hammering starts up again as if to hide the fact that a boy lays dying just the other side of Mulberry Row. A robin, dull and boring scampers along the ground, cocking his head for the damned worm it is ripping up from the ground after a time. Life goes about its own time. Clang. Clang. Clang. I see out the doorway that some white man with a long coat goes into the shack with a black leather bag.

"You think they be able to do something for Brown?"

"Hard to say, Tom."

Cary stands back at his place hammering hard as if what he did could be hammered out with just a few extra strokes and forced to be forgotten.

"They's all so scared of Lilly's whippings, Tom."

"Why shouldn't they be, Jamie?"

"How many whippings have you ever had, Tom?"

Tom does not try to answer me, but instead he dodges a bit. "How many whippings you had, Jamie?"

"How many whippings has any of them had?" Neither Tom nor I has an exact answer to that one. Then finally I offer, "More than enough. Maybe too many."

Chapter Twenty-Eight

Gray can't seem to get apart from me this morning. After what occurred a few days back there's not much contention hanging in the air about the nail shacks, just the hammerings that always sounds, none of the shouts or laughs at times.

However right now all appears quiet, no Tom, no nail boys. A dog barks, off a ways down Mulberry Row, maybe down at the end of the way but no where near me and Gray. The sound tastes strange and dreamed, just as the past handful of days have felt.

Gray does not pay any mind to any of it. He climbs onto the roof of the little tool shed staring up into the top of the old walnut and hackberry trees as if that mockingbird cannot wait to be in his twitchy claws. "Of course Massa Jeff's mocker, Dick, would be easy to catch, Gray – were you ever to be invited to the President's house."

Now the mocker's taken to chasing the squirrels, three in all, up into the higher branches. Gray takes it all in for a time but soon jumps for a fly he swats and grasps as if it were more precious than the world's finest piece of gold.

"Gray is sure acting strange." Not sure where Tom

has come from all of a sudden.

"No stranger than any other day he acts, Tom."

"Pa be back again this morning."

"He sure be close by since Brown nearly died. Still got a smashed head the rest of his life though."

Tom does not answer. He points to the nail shed where everyone who is supposed to be in the nail shed has started filing on in. Massa Jeff lingers uneasily just inside the doorway. He clutches his book and his ink pen as always at the spidery tall-legged table. The scene contains no trace of Lilly. But Cary remains as gone as Lilly. Odd.

"I have weighed out ninety pounds of nail rod this morning, boys," says Massa Jeff. His voice is trying to sound happy. "Today, let us see if we can make that waste pile far less than yesterday's. My tailor – our tailor – has got bright new peach shirts all ready for –"

"Where is Cary?" Interrupts one of the boys.

"You will not be seeing or hearing from him. Those who disrupt things as Cary did, get sold further south to the Carolinas or Georgia. And some day, God willing, western Florida, should Spain misstep."

Silence. None can top that with a question or declaration on anything. I smash my anvil with the hammer to straighten some curvy nail rod I've been fingering, ending any possibility of discussion. Only I still have a question or two. I heard your boy Tom here tell me your friend President Washington freed his slaves when he died, well, instructed his wife, Miss Martha in something called a will, to do so when she dies. Why can't you, Mr. President?

Old Jupiter tells me you, Massa Jeff, is always saying how we all are slaves, that you must count, ever as our own debt here on the little mountain. I do not know what debt is or how the devil he enslaves.

But I do know what liberty means and how words are cheap and I had Tom read to me over and over your words. Though no matter how many times I say them in my mind I cannot find their exact meaning.

Can the liberties of a nation be thought secure when we have removed their only firm basis, a conviction in the minds of people that these liberties are of the gift of God? That they are not to be violated but with His wrath? Indeed I tremble for my country when I reflect that God is just: that his justice cannot sleep for ever.

I, sir, kind slave master, according to Jupiter's name for you, do take comfort in your trembling – may God help me.

Chapter Twenty-Nine

As hot, smokey, mean, and nasty as this place may be – as this work may be – I call it my sanity cave too. I climb down in here when things without just get to be too much. All presses down on my mind. But I can be hammering away, clinking, clipping, cutting, hearing the clink of nail after nail into the pile and not have to think of the church bell clanging its holy metal-on-metal sound, instead of this unholy one in here from the Devil himself.

Shut up, just shut up, Mr. Peter, peter, peter out there with your clowny crest. You old tit bird and there goes the Carolina bird they called a wren down at Poplar Forest. Here no one bothers to call it anything. They're all too busy being industrious, making nails that pay for all the groceries at this place. Thank you,

Tom for that lump of a fact. Fact be truth some say. But how so? Fact is, I make more of these damned nails than anyone else and that should mean I am in truth the happiest. In truth it be no fact. But my full stomach right now ain't worth all the hours and hours of nailing I've done to cover the groceries of this whole Monticello kingdom.

"Sir?"

"Take some time, Jamie," says Lilly.

I want to ask him time for what? He interrupts.

"You ain't keeping them straight of a sudden and you makes so many so quick, Massa will have a bunch that ain't quite perfect."

I want to clank this hammer down somewhere else aside from this anvil with its helpless nail atop it, but I'm not Cary whom Massa shipped south as an example. I want to tell Lilly to get up off his lazy, fat white ass and make them straighter if that is how he wants them. I doubt he would last five minutes at this work. But that is irrelevant, as Tom told me. It is irrelevant that what some white man can or cannot do means nothing in this unfair world of slaves and free man.

Cool out here, I notice, when taking my leave of the shed at Lilly's suggestion. Good breeze. Anything, anywhere – even in the hottest of summer – is cooler than in that nail shed. "Peter. Peter. Peter. Yo ass – bird! Just quit!"

"Just quit what, Jamie?"

"Tom?"

"What?"

"I missed you, Tom. Where you been?" His body feels far more solid than it looks when I hug him.

"You are going to have to quit from that, Jamie."

"What for? Haven't seen you for too long." Tom is not himself, not one bit. By now he would have told me about every thought that passed through his mind just since lunch. As he used to say, I can't begin to cease all the thoughts come to me like a long steamy summer rain. I'm ready for some of that rain. This has been a cold March.

"You don't know anything do you, Jamie?"

"You mean nothing –"

"I mean anything, you fool."

"What are you saying, Tom?"

Tom picks up a chunk of nail waste that his pa didn't get to weigh and write into his damnable journal and flings it at the tit bird. The bird goes silent before slipping from sight behind a fence. "Do you know what the word banish means?"

"When you pull out your knife or your sword if you be one of them pirates you used to read to me about?"

"No, you simple man. That's brandish." He catches me closing my eyes for a long pained moment. "Sorry, Jamie. You don't hear all these fancy words like I did all these years out of his mouth. Well, banish means to be sent away, like Romeo in the play, the story of Romeo and Juliet when Romeo kills Juliet's first cousin Tybalt. Only in my case I be sent away because somebody wrote a pamphlet and a newspaper story that says I exist. I am the child not of a mother and father but of a white master and his black slave, his concubine – not my mama."

The telling empties me like a bladder drained of water. Sally Hemings is whiter than most white people here on the mountain. Were a stranger, a visitor, told of her being a slave, they would doubtless not believe such a claim. But she's still a slave in blood, though Massa's years-dead wife is her half-sister. I grab Tom and hold him from the back, hold him until he starts into collapsing. Sobs come on but make no sound despite the blare of Carolina wren and warning warblers and red birds down the way – below the mountaintop, this mountaintop, Monticello, little mountain, little mountain of big misery.

Chapter Thirty

It is quiet enough right now to hear the flap of the thrash bird feathers and then its tearing and thrashing about in the dried leaves on the other side of the fence. These sounds are just noise and joining them comes the mocker bird rising above all the other sounds, robin red-breasts, children's shout and cries, nail hammers below – where I've got to be soon – and the constant clop of the horses. One horse chooses to whinny cocky, silly and loud, a whinny for all the crap of this place for all the feelings swirling around out there but never acknowledged.

"He don't think I saw it."

"Saw what, Tom?"

"Just shut up, Jamie. Listen. Saw it, the number, or any of his carefully written notes to himself along with all the weights of those damned nails. Some of those nails even going in bushels to nail together the President's mansion up in the town what they name for the man what freed his slaves when he, no his wife, Martha, dies. Washington."

Tom stops and takes a long breath. He's grown up

so fine. Has his father's long pretty nose and those kind eyes of his father, but they are so much kinder and searching and understanding in Tom than in Massa Jeff. Massa's eye so reminds of blue-green ice rather than summer waters.

"What you thinking, Jamie? Quit looking at me that way. I got to tell you something. I be gone at two of the clock and you need avoiding a whipping or getting more of a quota so you get yourself some nice new shoes or that blue jacket for –"

"Stop it, Tom. Shut up. Ain't thinking about any of that. Thinking what a fine young man you is."

"You are, Jamie. Say it right, dammit."

"You are, Tom."

"That's mule shit. What's it matter? I could be his damned Apollo he always speaks about. He loves the fucking Romans, but I still be Tom the slave. And now, to save his arse, his President's job, I am banished from here and go to be Thomas Woodson, not Tom Jefferson as I should be or Tom Hemings, what others think of me as."

His word come tight and terse. Mocker bird replaced by a wheezy flock of cedar wax birds.

"What was it you said you saw, Tom?"

"You better get your arse down there. Hammering's letting up and –"

"No. They can beat me – but they won't, they never do – just tell me what you saw." I'm not leaving till he tells me. Birds sound like they want to know, gone pretty much silent as has all else.

Tom takes a deep breath, lets the air out real slow, eyes fix down on the smoke of the pretty little town growing up to the west, below this little mountain.

"Back in the year you come here, no maybe a year or more before it, 1793, I think, in the side margin he underlines the word four three times and notes that that four be the assured increase in profits for this plantation. Plantation. Such a fine-sounding word for hell. That profit be as long as there continue a regular increase in the birth of us slaves. And this ain't even affected by any of the deaths that may occur as well. Then he puts, 'this is surely substantial and well worth noting as well as most advantageous, point of fact, pointing to the need for advancement which my family has as its right.' Funny thing. While he was in France he come to admit to all those calling for liberty, that slavery has to go, though gradually. In the last 15 to 20 years that gradually has borne us 143 more slave souls added to our happy family."

Something about the sound of Tom's words gets to me more, even than what those words may mean.

"You didn't hear a word I just said did you, Jamie?"

"Heard 'em, Tom. Not sure of their meaning." Robin blasts the air with its warning cry as a mocker bird sounds as if he be trying to calm Mr. Robin down. Gray's probably stalking the bird around her nest.

"Jamie. Answer me. I asked you what you be thinking. No. Don't tell me. You are thinking about those damned birds again."

"Birds let me imagine a place where something does as it wills, Tom."

He sucks in another deep breath and I give it my full attention. I cannot stand the sound of his exhale when he is perturbed – another word he taught me, thanks to the pa what no longer claims his own son.

"Four. What did I say it means?"

"It be the increase, the percent increase as long as

babies are made by us slaves."

"You amaze me, Jamie." His eyes fix on mine.

"You think I don't understand, right?"

Tom nods slowly. But he is lost in thought. Then, with his eyes narrow, he looks past me, through me to somewhere else. "Duke de La Rochefoucauld-Liancourt. I always remembered that name as being the longest name I ever heard a person as having. For years I got old Massa Jeff to say it to me so I could know how to say it. One day not too long ago I asked about the duke from France's visit. 'My operations fascinated the man', explains Massa Jeff. 'He took an interest in my plowmen and women, gardeners, shepherds, millers, charcoal burners, sawyers, carpenters, cabinetmakers, wheelwrights, carriage makers, coopers, basket makers, nail makers, tinsmiths, spinners, weavers, dyers, seamstresses and tailors, shoemakers, brickmakers, bricklayers, stonecutters and stonemasons, glaziers, painters, roofers, midwives, candlemakers, coachmen, wagoners, brewers, soap makers and whatever else I may have here at Monticello. Then he smiled and wondered why that did not prove wrong my argument that slaves are children, who cannot fend for themselves and therefore cannot be emancipated, must not be freed the gradual way as I say it must go.'"

"So how did he go on from there, Tom?"

Tom's face darkens in a painful hopelessness what nearly tears up my eyes. "'The natural way always takes time he says, 'and they remain no less children. Even a monkey may parrot what a person does, a parrot ape the sounds it hears all about.'"

"Goose shit. There be but one creature I know what enslaves others in nature – aside from white men – and that be the cowbird and mostly that doesn't go

Peter Hildebrandt

well for the cowbird. Only a few of its babies can make a slave of its mother what ain't really its mother, say a Mama Cardinal, Mocker bird or Sparrow."

"The people here, white or otherwise, know nothing about how well you understand, Jamie."

"Good. That be the way I like it. I want them to think that be so."

"Tell me, Jamie, what you be thinking now?"

I pull him to me close and hold him a long moment. Then I pound his back with my flat palms. The slap sounds but hardly moves him. Tom's grown solid and firm, hard to move despite a lingering boy-scrawniness to him. How do I begin to explain? His revelations simply back up all the doubts building up a long, long time. "The groceries for this place be bought with the sweat and blood of those little nail boys – us nail boys. Your pa holds out a fine buckskin shirt with a collar, blue velvet trim and tie strings on it, shoes, gloves, and even a better position long as I make quota and make no trouble. But that number four be a number there every year, every year it grows, this all grows by factor of four as long as people what cannot leave for fear of their lives, procreate and – "

"Procreate? My, God Jamie you remembered that word?"

"I won't be bought with things, Tom. That four increase means there be more bought to drive me, bribe me. I would not have such things offered to me. I overheard one of Massa Jeff's guests speak using terms from card play. He pointed to a pile of finery on a pallet and said 'to quell rebellion among your slaves, that nice material shall ever be your trump card'. I do not go, will not fall for the false hope of trump."

"Then what do you have?"

I have said my piece. I am not talking anymore. Tom doesn't press me. He knows. Things are quiet down at the nail shed, praise the Lord. Boys to their sorry pallet beds, supper not even a memory – dried fish once again – instead of pork as the house slaves get – saves the Master his precious money.

"Here. Listen to this. Just found it in my back pocket. I copied these down from some of his copied letters he sends people. He always keeps the originals."

"That means the first one what he done?"

"Right. Shut up and listen, 'I allow nothing for losses by death, but, on the contrary, shall presently take credit four per cent per annum, for their increase over and above keeping up their own numbers,' And here in one letter I see he advises a friend of his, a neighbor here in the area who was fighting the cost of things he 'should have invested in negroes'. In times of the civil war with the English, when they come close by here, word got out they'd offer any slaves their freedom. A young slave mother here and her two little girls lit out and escaped. Though they died of the smallpox before the English could inoculate them – Massa never does that to us slaves here – he put in claim with the English, some have taken lately to calling the British, for years saying they owed him for his losses in the war, his assets – though they be but a young mother and her little girls."

Tom all of a sudden reaches up and grasps my forearm and wrist as well as my thicker arm further up toward my chest.

"Am I an investment, Tom?"

Tom's face screws up in amazement. "Where the hell did you learn that word?"

"Lilly always talks of wasted investment and I

heard it long before Lilly, when I was first learning and the nails weren't coming fast as the waste scrap metal littering the ground about my fire. 'How much more of that nail rod investment you gonna waste, Jamie, boy?'"

"You knew then, Jamie and what's more you even had me fooled. Were I a spy or smith I'd tell them to quit from their plan to let you make deliveries to town and beyond."

Chapter Thirty-One

Things are quiet here atop the wagon. Tom's words give me strength in some ways. I want to cry thinking about him being gone. I pound my chest. "You are still in here, in this strong heart o' mine."

Another wagon comes right up behind mine. I hear it, then turn around to see that it's a small carriage with two white ladies facing each other in the back. The driver nods his head. "Pretty new breeches, Sir. Jamie, correct?"

"Thank you, Sir." I stare at the back of the carriage after it passes. My horse still lumbers on as if their carriage was not even there. I search my mind to recall the man's name. Maybe he's one of Tom's cousins, lighter-skinned enough to be one of the 'white' guests up in the main house at Monticello. I rub the fabric of the knee britches. They're all mine. No one gave them to me. I stayed up all night burning charcoal and tending the kiln and making extra nails in the day just to get them. And knowing, thinking on all of that brings me right to the supply store.

"This be more bushels of wheat than I ever seen," says the man at the grain board. "How you get that old mount to move with this much stuff?"

I'm not sure what to say. No one has ever talked to me without hardly telling me to get moving here to go there, go somewhere else. "Sir, I figured a way to do it, move that horse some ways."

Clang. Clang. Clang. A solid sound of hammering throbs up from a big building down the way. I smell smoke and hear more hammering, deliberate and solid, not rushed and fearful like in the nail shed.

"You just start lately up at the President's place?"

His question surprises me completely. He thinks I am a free black. I cannot help but smile.

"What you smiling on? Mr. President tell you some story about his hating the last man what be president?"

"I do not hear much. He is not there much no more – anymore. I been on with the place a fair time." The words seem to shut down talk like an old trunk slamming shut for some reason. Not quite sure what he thinks now.

My horse gets lively heading back all of a sudden. A cat cries out from some alley. "Gray, you better not be down here in town. Horned owl get ya so far from home just like I might get grabbed if I wander off just a bit too far from my own nail shed." The horse sighs. I should have worn my hat and one of my two new overcoats. It is cold for spring. "Sorry, Tom. Said I could not be bothered with finery. Well I got it now. Just gotta keep 'em thinking that be enough for me."

Chapter Thirty-Two

Red birds trillin' a storm this morning. Most mornings I would not pay it any mind. But this morning – no – I need some peace. I stayed up nearly all night and got a bucket full of nails to show for it. Thanks Mr. Sparrow with the white throat. Needed that calming song of yours to get the red bird's crazy sounds from out of my head.

"You been right busy, Jamie." Gabriel Lilly's son, Wilson always manages to be around just when I'm wanting to get things steady.

"Yes, well I got lots of other things to do today, Wilson."

"I can tell you been up all night. No one could have that many nails, fresh off the fire and cut and hammered out without some time."

I want to tell him not a single person could do this in a week's time, let alone a night's time that is, except me. But he and his mean-arsed father already know that. Hell. Everyone knows it. "Why you think they gave me this place over here, all by myself, with none to distract me or take my time away?"

"You forget who you be talking to."

"I ain't ever forget who I be talking to, Wilson."

Gray comes over and looks up into my eyes, licking his mouth as if he's got what he needs for his gut somewhere. A rangy dog that has been hanging around awhile now comes over and sniffs the cat as I pet him. Now Gray's tail whips at me.

"That means he's agitated with you, Jamie. They don't whip they tail like that unless that be the case."

"What is agitated?"

"Means he be anxious, nervous, maybe a bit angry's the way I take it."

"How do you know all that?"

"I be up in his library plenty times with Pa when he's leaving his records up there. They be all kinds of books on stuff and they be mostly scattered all about on the floor more times than not. Guess it be a result of all that damned fiddle music you always hear up at that place. Massa Jeff rather do that and sing most the time instead of doing such as shelving up them books."

"You can read them?"

"How else would I know this stuff? I've read since I was seven. My ma and my brother been reading to me but that ain't good enough. I want to know the words, too."

I finish loading the wagon with the tools that need repairing in town, along with some of the extra greens they are going to sell. That, and wheat bushels I haul up there. Then I turn to face Wilson. "Can you write out words like them what you read?"

"Of course." I cannot gauge his reply. It's like Gray and his agitation in his tail. What does that answer, his tone mean exactly? I study his face. He has none of his father's hardness. Wilson is easy to get smiling but he is no fool either. Since Tom has been gone, Wilson seems to fit right into life like a glove that's just a tad too tight for doing much work around this place. "Well, what do you care if I can write or not?"

"Well, that this just be something good to know."

He stares up at me as I sit at the front of the wagon. "You want to ride with me?" My question surprises him and I am afraid it surprises me, even more.

"Let me get my jacket first and tell Pa."

"Nah. Don't bother telling him." My words tighten up his face somehow and when that happens I see his father in his mouth and eyes. Only I try hard not to let on that I do see this.

We travel along for a time. One man with a load on his back straightens up at the sight of us. Some of the kindling sticks he carries tumble to the ground. He struggles to get the load completely down on the ground and starts to rearrange the bundle. "Hallo – you two having a good old time?" He waves again.

"And you just made a whale of a lot more work for yourself, man," shouts Wilson turning around to stare at the man for a time.

"That I did. I ain't in no hurry. No one's gonna whip me if I don't get back to Mulberry Row any quicker than this," calls back the man. A smile spreads across his face.

I try to gauge his chuckle and whether or not he knows just who he spoke to with those words. Wilson seems not to hear them. But his blank look is about as helpful as looking into Gray's old cat face – a complete mystery.

"You look like you're moving even slower than me with my bones that don't even want to pretend they be young anymore." The old man at the warehouse shakes his head waiting for us to comment. I do not say a word.

"How old are you?"

"I am over 41years now?"

"You're not lying about being old," says Wilson. "We did have a good-sized load, old man."

I nod in agreement. "This be enough stuff for you to deal with, Mr. Luther.

"I'll be sure to credit Mr. Jefferson – Mr. President's account for all these nails, Jamie."

"Yes. Be sure to do that so – "

"Gonna give us something stating that – in writing?"

The words surprise Mr. Luther. He nearly drops a bushel of wheat at Wilson's question.

"I suppose I could do it, smart arse. Never done that for Jamie, here."

"Well that makes sense. He wouldn't be knowing what you write on the paper no ways."

Luther raises an eyebrow and studies my face. I look directly in his eyes and they be about as puzzled as Gray's eyes when he thinks I got something for him to eat in my pocket.

On the way back Wilson does not say a whole lot for me to hear. I can tell thoughts stream through his mind like the babbling of the creek. I am sure he thinks of all kind of stuff, maybe something to finally say to me.

"I was harsh back there, Jamie. I'm sorry. But there's no way of knowing if those nails what you made and carried to him be applied to the cost of the salt, molasses and all of the rest of the stuff in the back of the wagon now."

"What is this?" I hold my finger on something I heard called a word at one time.

"'Received' – that means that you brought him enough weight of nails that he applied this 15 dollars to the cost he charges for that food back there, those turkey eggs, for instance, the lard we had to buy seeing how we run out from that last hog slaughtering done."

Wilson appears younger than me and I could

easily crush his scrawny frame with one great squeeze. I'd probably break a mess of his ribs. But he showed his power in other ways this day. I do not know quite what to make of him, him and me. Or is it I? I miss Tom. He would know what to say. I cannot even write to him. "Would you help me write a letter to Tom, Wilson?"

"Hemings?"

"He be called Woodson now and lives over the western lands of Virginia."

"Just tell me what to write, Jamie."

I feel better of a sudden. Air sucks into my chest. Feel as relaxed as when Gray sprawls cross a thick flat hickory tree limb, one paw just dangling.

Chapter Thirty-Three

Clang. Clang. Clang. The hammer fits down here, fits like it never did over in the main shed by Mulberry Row, where all those others still slave away. Slave. Funny word. You can use it to be something you do or you can use it to be something solid like me – and I am solid. Lilly doesn't need to check on me. He's got his damned bucket of nails each day and I notice it's gone first thing in the morning.

Gray likes to sit on that table and let his tail brush across my arm at times. But overall I want to toss him outside. He must be deaf by now. This clanging doesn't seem to bother him near as much as it used to.

"Looking right civilized in here, Jamie." Sounds like something Wilson would say.

"I got my work to do. Do not bother me, Wilson. Do not want Lilly – your pa – to come and whip me like he does them little boys."

"That's thanks you give me for my helping you with –"

"And I don't help you?"

"Do you have a choice?"

The words sting. The truth here, off from Mulberry Row out in the quiet, otherwise lovely woods still bites far worse than Gray's biting my leg this morning with his tomcat anger. He sits now facing the open doorway, ears flipping out to catch sounds that must be ones impossible for us simple humans to be hearing.

"I choose to help you out, Jamie. I don't have to, you know."

"I choose not to hold my hands around your –"

"Watch it, Jamie."

Something in the way his eyes flash at me. Is that a wink? Yes, there I am once again. Clang. Clang. Clang. "Fan that flame, Wilson, could you please?"

"Since you asked all nice and friendly – no hard feelings – I can do that. Got some news you might want to hear."

"Thank you, Sir. What might that news be?" The noise of my hammer has stopped and now the smoke has too much fanning by Wilson, and it's hard to breathe in here a spell.

I walk to the door. Red birds cover the hillside with their honey sweet songs, wrens and a half dozen other bird sounds find their way all throughout the hills above me.

"Tom's done married some girl named Jemima."

"Good for Tom. You gonna help me write him

another letter, Wilson?"

That wink again. I want to ask him about other stuff, friends – not his damned pa – brothers, sisters, his ma, where he came from before here. But I figure anything beyond what he already says be a gift to me."

"Why do you like cats, Jamie?"

"I don't. I like dogs. Cats, well certain cats, Gray for example, just like me."

"You got some nice things now, Jamie, real nice."

True. But I don't say another word about that comment. "'Dear Tom, I am glad you found somebody what would marry you' – got your paper and quill, Wilson?"

"Why don't I ever see you wearing these nice things, this buckskin coat here, fringes and everything? Not a spot on it and here it be you never wear it."

"One right behind it even nicer, Wilson. You like them? Which one you like the best?"

"This one would be perfect – "

"You can't have it, at least not yet."

Wilson stares down at the pages he brought over just like I do. Ink's already dripped onto the table, but not on the paper, not a single drop.

"What's that up there?"

"Told you already. That be called the salutation."

"Big word for a little 'Hallo'." He knows what I do. If I do not think of something else to say soon, he's gonna be gone to find something more interesting to do himself.

"They call this writer's block, only you have it, not me and you can't even write a word. All right, Jamie. I'll get you started. It has been fine weather that we been having here – how about by you?"

Wren bird blasts out his tea kettle – tea kettle – tea kettles and I want to do the same. But Wilson has written something. It is nothing I would write, but it is something.

"'Place not been the same since you been gone, my friend' – did you get that?"

Drink your tea bird, Tom called the tow hee or joree and the lonesome white-throat sparrow song all fill my mind enough to make it explode with thoughts, things that I want to tell Tom.

"All right. I got that. If you don't come up with more than that you will have one short letter."

Two chickens at the edge of the woods see which one of them can scream louder to announce their just-laid eggs. I go and pull a fat black snake from the dark corner by the door to the chicken coop, chop off his head with the end of a busted hoe and watch as several yellow eggs drain from his body. Damned dog, I think, when I get back to Wilson. I wonder if that is why I have not seen Gray around in a while. "Quit your barking. We be trying to write to Tom in here."

"How about 'How things working out at your new place?'"

"Right, and 'I heard you got married. What would that be like, Tom?'"

That damned dog wants to tear up old Gray. "Just leave him be. He is worn out from being a lady's man all night, Wilson."

"Should I put that in the letter?"

"Better put something. 'I miss you, Tom. What is it like being away from here, being able to come and go as you please, able to find someone to marry and know they ain't gonna someday just take them away from you, be putting them up on the block to be sold like a horse?'"

Chapter Thirty-Four

Could I write, dear Tom, I wouldn't ask you about the weather like I do when Wilson takes down my words to you. I got your letter the other day and it is so good to hear from you.

No. I am just sitting here done with my work for the day. More than 11 pounds of nails done, good enough for any of them. At least no one is complaining. But sitting doesn't go on for more than a moment as I've got my eggs to gather up and garden to work for planting sweet potatoes. None of those nail boys can live on dried herring from Massa Jeff each week. They would starve if they tried. Though to listen to him a body would think they would starve if he weren't there to feed them. What mule shit. They'd starve were it not for me and the old slaves and chillins too young to do anything else but working the garden and the chickens.

I would just truly write to you dear Tom how much I miss you. That sounds womanish and corny but it is the truth. I watched you growing up alongside me from a skinny boy like me to a good solid young man. No surprise the first thing you did was to go get married.

You are right in that letter. I've got a fine thing given to me for my hard work. Means about as much as this piece of sour apple I just scooped up off the crate and took the last bite from, good while it is going down but soon forgotten.

When all is quiet-like as right now, with just the clucks and endless scratchings of my chickens going on and I go on dreaming these words what form in my mind I can put to page, just like Wilson does, I want to ink you the truth. The truth is I do not care about any of it, none of the stuff, none of the extra fancy food, clothes, or beer they give me, none of it.

What do I care about you ask? Fair question, Tom. Remember how you used to ask me questions all the time about how I got my nails so perfect and quick and what my family was like? I almost cry this night just thinking about that. As if I have no family. Can hardly recall what they look like.

I remember you yet or though or whatever the word is supposed be and how much you love the father who isn't a father of yours and who sent you away. You could probably read between the lines of this letter of mine I form in my head, squeeze the apple till the juice drips out into a sweet cider and drink in its meaning.

There is no point to living if your life is not yours. I still recall Colonel Randolph's face when he told the story of that neighbor's slave. His massa came out first thing in the morning to see that slave hanging high up in a shagbark hickory tree. Massa Jeff say it be an act of a coward to end one's life. Massa Jeff's son-in-law, the colonel has no part of it. He says he's seen nothing braver than taking back the life that never was yours to live, turns on his heels and will have no more talk of Jeff or Lilly or anyone else.

Doesn't anyone know this? Each brick in your pa's house, the President's house isn't just a brick. That earthen rectangle – thank you Tom for the fancy words – stands for sweat and hard bloody labor with no pay, forced work what some other body gets the gain from. It isn't pretty. It is a wall that traps me forever and I aim to climb it, Tom – be gone, come what may.

No, Wilson. You aren't ever gonna see this letter from out of my mind, not for any amount of cornbread bowls piled high with pork fat and bacon or that fancy bourbon they gave me one Sunday, thinking I can be bought with something that may matter to some of the others. But no, those thing do not matter or concern me, James Hubbard.

Chapter Thirty-Five

All I hear this morning is the red bird with his what-cheers about me to make me deaf. And yesterday I heard a flock of Carolina parrots with their squawks. I can kiss my fingers to make a like sound and the bright green and yellow birds go silent as if I am some kind of a bird slave-catcher. I smile. Massa Jeff is enraged by the parrots. But they are just like him. They profit from the work of others, attacking all the hard work of the gardeners with their apple orchards and leaving the fruit to rot on the ground while they go for those little brown seeds inside the fruit.

"Can't you make this thing to move any faster, Jamie?" asks Wilson, his face as expressionless as that of a Carolina parrot.

"They are moving fast as they feel they need to go, Wilson. Got that letter to Tom?"

"You need to quit asking me that, about that damned letter."

Now there are red birds on one side and the other. A break comes. But then the tea kettle wren wants his say. "All right. Just stop, all you birds. Fly away for a change."

"They don't do it this time of year, Jamie. Something called being 'territorial.'"

"What the hell does that mean?"

"They're calling out their place telling others what think they might want in around their nest, that that moving by another bird ain't a possibility."

All while he is saying that, I go on thinking just the opposite for me. I want to be announcing my territory isn't anywhere near here. "Tom is smart. He got his own territory – anywhere but here."

"Tom be like a competing male bird only his has to do with someone saying truth about his parentage, who his true ma and pa be."

"Tom always told me his ma be Miss Sally. And we both know who his pa be, though you never would hear that claim come out from his pa's lips. Then, later on Tom told me his ma never was nor ever would be a wife – she be but a concubine. What does that word mean? You ever heard it said?"

"Coming from outta the mouth of Tom, who knows? I always thought a concubine be something, someone from those Orient lands such as China would have. Abraham had a concubine and a wife. His son Jacob had two of each. But Massa Jeff never takes no mind of the bible nor ever says things from out of the book. So who knows?"

"Tom said Massa Jeff courted his first wife, Martha. But he never did that with Miss Sally, though they are half-sisters. Miss Martha's father had Sally through Betty Hemings. Miss Betty told Tom that her father, a Captain Hemings be willing to purchase her when she be a little thing and raise her up free as his own declared daughter, but old Martha's father, Massa

Wayles, would take no money no matter what the price, didn't want her to be free, be called any white man's daughter. And Miss Sally could have run free when she be in France as keeping slaves be unlawful there. But Massa Jeff told her if she comes back to Virginia and be his slave, his promise to her was that her children and she would be given their freedom."

"No sign of that happening anytime soon, Jamie. Though they do have it much easier than the field slaves down below the house."

"Still, that be a long ways from free."

Flies buzz around the melons that have softened up in the back of the wagon. I do not see how they expect to sell them. The nails do not jingle when we hit the ruts today. Means that is a fuller bucket than last week.

"You gone quiet, Jamie. What are you thinking now?"

"I be wondering how good you truly be at writing a letter, one what could convince someone of something." A pair of dogs takes it upon themselves to crush my words just as they come from my mouth. One dog barks. The other one has to prove he can bark even louder. They're not even looking at us movin' along the road behind their yard. Dogs just live in some other place, nose to the sky, taking it all in.

"I can write whatever needs to be written, Jamie. Haven't you sent enough letters to Tom lately?"

I do not know how to put what I want to say next. I do not feel like I know Wilson completely. We ride to town to deliver supplies, bring my nails, my hard work, and take the money back. It all feels right and normal and all together. It is for Wilson. Would be right for him. Only it isn't for me."

"I still don't know what you mean and – "

"Just shut up a minute. I hear some gunshots and a pack of dogs. Hear them?"

"Must be an escape, Jamie. Dogs get that frenzied sound when they be egged on in a group like that. That is their work and they love being in the thick of it."

"And I do hate it."

Chapter Thirty-Six

It is good not to smell the smoke that swallows up the from nail shed, for a change. Instead, the earth dampens my feet at least until I have to go back and let them know I still work on the nails. I do not think of anything else. No.

How could I possibly think of anything else? I am a machine and they do not think I know anything else. These hands, these arms, these legs and thighs – stronger than most belonging to anyone for miles around. They are not even mine. They belong to –

"Did you get your quota for the day, Jamie?"

"No. Not today, Wilson."

"Well what are you doing sitting out here all by yourself?"

The morning is chilly though spring is well under way. Gray was so insistent so wanting me to feed him some of that food – food I no longer have – that I put him up in the tool shed.

"I heard your cat on the way over here, Jamie."

"I get to needing some peace, even from him." I look up and hold his gaze.

"You need to be finishing up your – "

"Damn the quota. Your pa gonna beat me, gonna whip me?"

The red bird trills hard and then all goes silent for what feels like hours and Wilson, staring at my forearms and shoulders for some reason, goes quiet, too. An oddity. That boy never seems to shut his mouth at times. No. Spoke too soon.

"No. I ain't gonna – no – Pa ain't gonna whip you, Jamie."

"Good. Look at your arms, Wilson, scrawny as Gray's. Why don't you make some nails for a change?" The question makes about as much sense to him as if I'd asked him to go ahead and move to Algeria. And the only reason I know that word is that he told it to me regarding something that Massa, – no President Jefferson – had to say about something. A distant freight team horse, slaves in their own way, screams and whinnies. "Wilson, I need you to do something for me. I got some money for you and that best jacket of creamy buckskin, fringed and trimmed material what you favor, for you."

"Gray's gone and got out. Look. He's under your hand-carved chair."

"Did you even hear me? I'm not talking about Gray."

"I heard you. I'll do it. You know I will. Don't want them hands of yours around my neck – ever."

"I don't quite know how to take that. Do not say such as that."

The birds that pass through this time of year twitter and wheeze and stretch out their sweet, sweet, sweets. And those chimney swifts twitter on the breezes above as well. Perfect day, all except for my restless head.

"You got everything here, Jamie. Your pick of the food just yonder, all yours for the taking and all the clothes you might ever ask for – you are cared for. Why would you want to go and leave all of this? I don't understand."

"No. You do not understand." I stare down at the ground to try to make him understand why I am having him write that letter claiming to be a free man. I think of the fireflies that quit their glowing when they are bottled up. I should not waste that idea on him. I think of the words that Tom told me he read of Massa Jeff's fears of us slaves rising up in a murderous slave rebellion.

We have the wolf by the ears and feel the danger of either holding him or letting him loose. Yet I recall, too, that the one who claimed slavery must end certainly finds a multitude – thank you, Tom for that word – of uses for us slaves. But these also be jobs that sure do not feel like anyone is heading to freedom: nail-making, tin smithing, carpentry, cabinetry, fine French cooking, blacksmithing, wagon and tool making for the new wheat needing harvesting. Then I think of what Wilson heard his pa tell him when Massa Jeff speaks of a letter from some kin thinking of freeing their slaves. Old Jeff says it would never do to destroy the goose! Goose? I thought we were the wolf, us slaves. Could he mean that goose instead that lays those golden eggs?

All of a sudden I hear the bird what sounds like it laughs at the world with his screeching sounding little bursts. I know his little harem of two lady birds is not far off.

"First cowbird I've seen this year," says Wilson.

"Right. You know what they do, do you not? They will lay their eggs in the nest of another bird so that bird has to raise them."

"I ain't stupid."

"Well, who knows about that? How is that bird any different from what you white people do? I was not born enslaved, really – born no different than you. But that egg you people laid in my life keeps me from helping myself. That egg kills my own young by their never being born and gets you, your pa, Massa Jeff and all the rest something for never having to lift a finger or arm. Well maybe it gets lifted just to beat me when you do not get enough out of me. I see one o' them tiny warblers and a sparrow once, fighting to feed that cowbird baby twice its size. Ain't never enough food it seems. Ain't never enough slaves. We still oblige with our babies, though."

"I wouldn't be saying those kinds of things, Jamie, not while Massa Jeff or Pa are about – not if you know what's good for you."

Chapter Thirty-Seven

I did not leave my door open. Not that I can remember. With the fire going and the door to my nail shed closed, there be some time – a day maybe – before they realize I am gone. I got the papers that Gabriel Lilly's son, Wilson, dared to write up for me.

Wilson did not know when I would be going. Not a clue. He is so irregular in his comings and goings that noticing could take a whole week. My jacket looks good. He's got the newer one now. Knowing Wilson, he isn't gonna be wearing it in front of anyone for a long time. I do not know exactly where this road goes. I've been on it just about all night.

Yesterday I got a ride in a wagon from somebody who did not even ask to see any papers. This gives me hope, no faith...one or the other. But right now it is chilly, real, real chilly for April. Yes. All the regulars are singing – red bird, white throat and some other bird with a sound like a machine I could imagine Tom telling me his pa invented.

I close my eyes and see Gray sitting on the arm of my chair pretending to be a statue. Right now I feel about as frozen as a statue. So cold. I want to get from this cold and find some – "

"Well, now that's a long ways to be walking when there ain't no place to go for miles." The voice startles me and I turn to see a man on horseback.

"I do not mind the walking."

"Get on. I'll get you a bit further. I'm going about another nine miles. Nice jacket. Real pretty. Don't suppose it gives you much heat this morning."

"No, really does not warm me, much." For a horse as small as his, there really is quite a bit of room, I notice as I jump on the back. The horse shudders once I am on. I am a good bit larger than the other man. His strange plain collar with a white part showing at the front and wide-brimmed hat make me think he is one of those folks who Tom told me visit Montciello from time to time, Shakers or maybe it is Quakers.

"You look like you are lonely. But too, you look like you know exactly where you want to be."

"Not sure quite what you mean by that, Sir," I reply.

"Well, then, we shall leave it at that and enjoy the morning. You got me to thinking about this whole strange institution we have to deal with each day we live here in Virginia. For someone who used to complain about the slaves, the President, just up the road there, sure does little to rid us of the scourge."

I nod in acknowledgment, but only a slight motion. He squints back at me all of a sudden, as if there is a dawning in his mind that the fact is I have not a clue as to what he is talking about.

"A few months back when I revisited Monticello I noticed Jefferson now has the roads at the place arranged differently," the man continues. "You ride up to the house and see only woods, as if the mansion before you came from some wave of a magic wand. Slaves and all associated with them are now completely hid from view. And in this Louisiana Purchase, the President has now bestowed upon us, slaves are completely allowed, in perpetuity. You ever been to Monticello?"

"Been meaning to go and see the place sometime," I say keeping my voice as flat and even as I can. "I just haven't had the time," I lie.

"I'm not saying it isn't a lovely place, exactly, just that 'tis constantly remodeled, on the backs of the slaves. They must surely think it ironic they're forced to work on the home of the man who put ink to parchment to bring life to something called the 'Declaration of Independence'."

"I have heard it told there is some work goes on there with iron, such as nail-making and black smithing to make tools for cutting the wheat he's just started in to growing, though I never had seen it with my eyes."

His chuckles go on for some time. Finally he laughs aloud. "Guess we could say 'tis ironic that iron be hard and ironic just a word with no metal nor hardness to it. In the end 'tis actions that count, not words and Mister – no – President Jefferson showed us as strong as a rainstorm that his words in his declaration may just be about as meaningful as the ink which that same rain would soon wash away as if it never existed. 'They are equal to the whites' says he, adding, but 'in imagination they are dull, tasteless, and anomalous...in reason much inferior'. Jefferson in turn finds it impossible to find a black person 'capable of tracing and comprehending the investigations of Euclid'. I ask you how many white Virginians, white citizens of any of the colonies – excuse me – states, could comprehend old Euclid? And don't you bother trying to give me an answer here. That 'tis something called a rhetorical question. I keep harkening in my mind back to observations of a man called John Stuart Mill, who stated, 'was there ever any domination which did not appear natural to those who possessed it?'"

The man's words baffle me. I recall Tom telling me about the Independence Declaration. This man does not think much of those words that Massa Jeff wrote. I think this Quaker preacher speaks the truth.

The roads and trails have been changed around Monticello. I never thought that such change as that may be to make us slaves unseen – what Tom defined as this word, invisible – to visitors. I also want to tell this man what a pretty morning it is, even if colder than any late April morning I can remember. Want to explain how I left my cat at home, how I could use a cup of coffee more than I can say, some eggs, honey, bacon, a boiled sweet potato from right out of my little garden patch.

"How is that for a smell?" asks the man.

Thoughts come to life. Maybe he is thinking the same thing. But certainly he smells the bacon frying. He lifts an arm and points down to a cabin along the river. "I'll get us some. You like bacon? Best maybe if you wait there." He points to a cove in the woods beyond the road. I'm not sure what is going through his mind. But the powerful smell of bacon, near to burning up, on the cold breeze blows away my fears of the moment.

Chapter Thirty-Eight

This is hard. Been days on the road now. The bacon retrieved from master Quaker was the best I have ever tasted. Had the best and the worst of people. Had to use the brain God gave me to figure out something, anything, to say each time, to each one.

Now this looks to be some sort of tobacco barn. The sweet smell of the stuff soaks into the very ground, air and wood all about me. There is a teacher, teacher, teacher wren. No, up here it sounds more like birdie, birdie, birdie. It seems annoyed with the sugary smell of curing tobacco as I am.

What you doing, Jamie? Where are you going? Each night I find the great drinking gourd, find the tip on the other end and how it points to the handle of the little gourd and as Tom used to say that way is always north, north, north where the states don't have no slavery –

"What you doing sitting around here? Don't you need to be to your work?" A lady in a long dress is followed by a little girl, maybe 14 and a boy, skinny, who must be 'bout 11. Evidently I have found myself on the border of their place.

"What's he doing here, Mama?"

"That's what I'd like to know," states the lady.

"I am heading to Richmond, Ma'am. You should have a right nice egg harvest with that basket of yours."

"How does he know we got eggs in our b. morning, Mama?" the boy asks in nearly a whi.

"Oh, I been around chickens for year. makes that sound what says to the whole worle. I just laid me an egg' and that's it. You got one – no – you got you a whole basketful if you just go a lookin' for the rest, and that be a pretty basket you got, Ma'am."

"You best be heading to Richmond then, as you said."

The thought of fresh eggs from the sound of all the chickens in the little shed next to that old tobacco barn, brings water to my mouth. I think of something Tom wrote in one of his letters, remember, Jamie, when white folks say justice, they mean just-us. Not exactly sure what that means but I do know right now that any eggs here are just for these white folks. I gather up my bag and put a finger to the edge of my hat as if to go.

A blew-jay flutters boldly down close to my feet to gobble up a caterpillar worm it spies there. I can hardly believe its nerve. Something in that pushes me. "For passing the time with me and letting me think on all those chickens and their eggs, I would like to split all that wood in the pile. That ax looks to be hardly used lately." The blue jay nerve of the offer settles my heart from its racing. Just this woman and her children here right now. That is all there is to the family, or there could be overseers inside ready to rope me down.

"Well, that would be first rate. Split the wood as you say and I will ring that bell on the porch when I fry up some of those fresh eggs."

"Can you give the man some potatoes too and a tin of coffee, Mama?" asks the boy.

I want to hug the little boy but instead I just watch the blue jay hop soundlessly up into the lower branches of the Catalpa tree as if to wink, "Now that is how you do it, Jamie."

Chapter Thirty-Nine

Tom would not believe where I am now. This situation I'm in, situation one of the words he liked to use when he would stop and just look around at this crazy world of ours. After days out along the road, I settled in this crowded farm, where I could blend right in with others.

Cold. So cold this morning and it is near to being May. At least that is what I heard one of those men who manage these work crews say.

My corner of the shed is quiet. There is a creamy white cat with orange and tan splotches, that rubs on my feet in the mornings. Then, I hear the others. Mainly they are silent but for their feet on the ground. They line up to plant the tobacco sprouts. I blend in easily with them, no problem at all. One wiry boy shadows me these days. Speak of that devil. He is back once more.

"What you say your name was?"

I'd known his name for days. Never met an Edgar before. "My name be Georgie, Edgar."

"How did you remember my name?"

"How could I forget?"

Birds mostly sound far, far off out here in this field. A ruckus raises up from the corner. Bodies block my way. I push in around the crowd to have a look with Edgar and all the rest. Some poor boy who looks to have fainted lies face down in the dirt. The overseer at this place has taken it upon himself to beat him awake.

"I got work to do." The others agree with their feet and follow me back to the corner where we have been planting. Besides, I am cold. I get colder with such a spec, specta. Tom told me the word once, spectacle as that. "You know what a spectacle is, Edgar?"

"Can't say that I do. I will say that I think sometimes you talk too much – "

"And sometimes, Edgar you thinks too much – "

"Damned worms!"

"You mean caterpillars, Edgar."

"When did you go and become President Jefferson, knowing everything?"

The irony – yes, Tom told me the meaning of the word – of Edgar's statement brings a smile to my lips. Then chopping up the sweet low-growing violets to make room for the damned tobacco sprouts, my smile dissolves just as quickly. I think of the humor of my situation. Here, an escaped slave passing as a real slave so he isn't caught by his original owner or shall I say owners.

As if to put voice to the silliness of it all, a goldfinch bursts across the field with his hill and valley laughing flight. Sun catches his gold and black like jewels. I feel like I am a boy once again, deciding out of all the feathered creatures that exist, that can fly to freedom as this gold finch which takes the most joy in that flight and shows it off for all to see.

"You got to get it all. Can't be leaving those little purple flowers, just 'cause they be pretty."

I want to ask Edgar if he knows anything. Could he be that simple that he does not know the name of a violet?

"That dog don't like you, Georgie," whispers

Edgar.

The dog keeps barking in my direction from the edge of the field. Overseers look from the dog directly to me and hold their gazes a long moment.

"Georgie? Your name is Georgie, ain't it...why don't you answer?"

"Oh, yes, Edgar. That be my name. Sorry." Dog still barks. Want to go crack him on the side of his head with this hoe. Take a breath, Jamie. Suck in a deep one. I do, and I smell the sweet sound of fresh cut grass and earth all to make way for more of that noxious tobacco weed about to be planted. Yes, Tom, noxious is another one of your word gifts to me, though not a pleasant word from what you told me. Clover lies all about, mixed with the grass. Makes me think of you again, Tom. Being boys lets us have some measure of free-ness, always looking for that four-leafer among the clover – when not making nails with the other boys.

"Georgie! Georgie, I'd wake up if I were you. Georgie?"

I hear Edgar's words as if in a dream for some time, a dream where I'm not anyone, in fact, I do not even know my own name. Too hot in here and my eyes open to the blackness.

"Ok. You awake," whispers Edgar. "I've been getting things ready for the tobacco's planting. I smelled coffee at the overseer's shed. Got you some. You gonna need it."

I sip the black liquid and nearly spit it out. Never take mine with sugar and this is nearly all sugar. "Why thank you, Edgar."

"Better drink up – fast. Here's a biscuit. Gonna need that too. You need to be out of here – and your name ain't Georgie."

"Yes it –"

"No. I heard the sheriff on his horse talking about them looking for someone goes by the name of 'James' or 'Jamie'."

"Sheriff?" I down all I can of the hot coffee, nearly choking on the over-sweetness and cram the biscuit in my mouth. "Thank you, Edgar."

"God bless you, Jamie," says Edgar.

The words take me by surprise. I hear the robins singing their tiny bird hearts out as if the sun will only come up if their voices are loud enough to bring that to pass. Drink your tea towhee bird and the teakettle wren gets me anxious to be moving. I do not look back. No need to see where I've been. All I got is what's ahead. I tie my jacket around my waist – too hot to wear.

Whatever town I am in has a church not wealthy enough to own some loud bells. They're tolling out of the gloom and blackness as if they are on my butt too. To add to my misery, I hear the howling of a pack of bloods. They're the dogs I hate most nearly as much as foxhounds.

I hear water. Some kind of creek cascades below. I strip off my shoes and tie them into my jacket. Rocks round, slimy as hell slip me up. Blackberry brambles cut my cheeks. I do not care. As long as I keep moving upstream those damned dogs cannot track me in the water. Scents float downstream if there even are any for them to toy with. For some reason out of the darkness I picture Gray, sitting there at the top of the stairs as always, staring at me as if asking just what the hell I'm doing. I hear a cat's meow up on the bank. "What the hell you doing here, you crazy animal?" I whisper. "Only thing you get outta this place is drown. You must be younger than Gray. Ain't got a lick of sense. Have you got a lick of sense, Jamie – or Georgie who cannot even remember when you heard your made-up name?"

Chapter Forty

I hear the bloods. They move in close now. This sounds like the racket of something that can go no further and knows it is licked. Of course, the creek has soaked my trousers right to the skin. But it is worth the price.

Now the breeze picks up and rain starts up as well as if to emphasize – Tom's word, not mine – my misery. I like that word. It fits right now. What, Jamie have you left to lose now? No clothes, no food, lost your hat and cannot get another until something else happens that causes you to have to get another hat. Hell. I even lost my Gray, my worthless worm-filled cat. Worms eating the thing up from inside out and were I to be back there I would probably not even recognize him. I like that word. Cannot remember if Tom taught me that one or not.

But I did lose something I am most grateful to lose – those bloodhounds. They dragged them back to their pens so they can lick their wounds after they have eaten their mess of food for the day. Lord. I am hungry enough to eat whatever it is those dogs have thrown to them.

I hear a veery-bird. Tom or maybe his father, the President told me about that one long ago. You hear the notes going steadily down, like they are drifting into a deep cool well. But I will be damned if I can see the bird, especially in this gloom.

The thick pine trees I worked my way up to, a

good ways above the creek, have made a good place for resting. I have got a fire going with my flint and iron and these pine needles and black birch bark to make the flames glow. But now I need to keep the fire low.

I open my eyes all of a sudden after dozing off to sleep for a time. The laughing and talking I saw in my dream, from something along Mulberry Row, was not just from Mulberry Row but here, wherever this might be. I grab some branches and rocks and smash out the fire, hating every minute of that as my clothes were just starting to toast up enough to dry off.

In the gloom of the early dawn I check the pages that Wilson wrote for me and the ink has not run. Words remain fixed, solid and strong on the dampening parchment paper. These are my pages to freedom. I thank scrawny old Wilson for doing that one thing for me, forming words on some pages, sheets of paper inked with symbols for making a man's life his own once more.

Inside my mama's belly I am free, no body owns me there, not even President Jefferson despite what he may have writ. Then when my bones lay beneath these dirt chunks, pine cones, pine needles, and clay earth – I do not belong to anyone but Mother Earth once more. Little comfort this gives me no matter how calming and poetical that might sound to all else.

Chapter Forty-One

"What experience have I got?" The question makes my head swim worse than if I had to cross the old James River.

"Well, if you can't tell me something for that

question why should I even try you out?" asks the man. He does not seem to have a name as much as own a color and the color red is his. He does not really look up from his anvil where he is hammering out an iron gate rod. He flashes a sideways glance my way amid the sparks.

"Yes, I have some smithing experience, making tools, er –"

"What sorts of tools you make?"

"Well, not really tools, nails, something you use with certain kinds of tools."

"I don't make no nails here. Got all I need from that fancy house, the place of the President up on his mighty hill he calls a mountain, Monty..."

"Monticello."

He looks up at me with another sideways glance lighting up his face all of a sudden. I no longer want to talk to him. My mind races ahead to further questions of his and my struggling to nail together a half-cracked answer without sounding ridiculous. "I take my leave now, Sir. I am sorry to have interrupted your work."

"You've not interrupted anything. I take my tea right at this time each day. Care to join me, Mr...."

"Mr. George – er – Woodson."

"Mr. Woodson."

"I thank you for your kind offer." There is nothing more to say or do, despite how much I would love to have some tea and those apple biscuits whose warm smells fill the air and that his wife or daughter has set out here. They look ready to fall to the dirty floor as they balance on a poorly-built table near the door.

"Goodbye then, Woodson."

I tip my nonexistent hat. Feeling foolish the

instant my finger taps my forehead. Lord, you know all our ways, all his – this smith's ways – give me strength to not fret over his face when I fought to say a false name to him. I feel just a bit better now.

Cold air has replaced the false warmth of earlier this morning and this quiet engulfing me has me antsy, a word the ladies at Master Jeff's loved to toss all around describing this person or that. Hammering from the smith shop I just left sounded steady and smooth. Deliberate, thank you, Tom. I like that word but the poundings also sound nothing like the sounds of Mulberry Row, at the nail shed, my nail shed. That's the one where I smash, hammer, straighten, clip, cut and crash iron on iron some more for hours on end. Wham, wham, wham, wham, just so I can walk outside in the grass with no shoes on for a few minutes and look down at the clover trying to find that lucky four. Four. Four leaves. And why are four leaves on a clover lucky?

Been thinking much about Master Quaker's words of some time back. I would be luckiest if Massa Jeff would maybe write about something else rather than what interests him. Of course, he is writing and going on and on about us blacks being inferior – I know what that means now – and that is a reason we are better off as slaves. But something sticks in this old head of mine, that writers write about what interests them. It interests old Jeff to keep writing about all these things that slaves give him, but all these things too, that he takes credit for. If we are not real folks, as he keeps writing, then I suppose – in his mind – we don't need to be thanked or acknowledged, paid or freed. My lucky clover in this life is that Jeff steps out of his room and writes what he does not know, all about me.

Those four-leafed clovers are like me, Jamie, here in this world of free life, free birds, free men and ladies. Something we, we slaves are always searching for, hoping for yet not ever having the thing we want the most.

"What's that sign say, Mama?"

The voice startles me with its urgency and with the fact that it does not ask about me, who I am, a black man walking down the –

"The sign says, 'Wanted: One tall slave, late of Charlottesville, reward may be offered. Inquire at the President's residence in Washington City.'"

I turn at the words and cross the muddy road without looking sideways to see if they even noted my reaction. At once I feel like old Gray, brushing up against my ankles and even jumping in my lap, head on my feet, tail high to keep every single inch of his body in contact with mine. I want a body in contact with mine. That is only, if only it might be to look that person directly in his eyes, drink in the sound, smell, taste and touch of his thoughts and feelings.

Rain starts up once again as my heart gets back to more steady in its course of beating. The drops patter on my shoulders and soak my head and hands. No where to go in the rain, no where to head to keep dry.

I find an old overhang at some abandoned out building and sneeze when the air, moist and dusty at the same time, irritates my nose. It feels good to clear out my chest, my lungs, use my body involuntarily without somebody's telling me I have to use it in a certain way. That going along with when they want me to use this body of mine in a certain way and how they want me to use it.

A rickety old rocker leans against the wall. I grab the thing and sit down in the murky light. Despite barely having eaten a thing all day long, I still feel full.

Waiting. I am just waiting. I rock and let the

sounds of the drips soothe me. They are out there. I hear the voices of children voices filling the gloom with far-off, matter-of-fact laughter. But just as Gray could see the shadows of other man-cats, hear their desperate screams in battle when I could barely be aware of all that, I know that people I haven't ever met or who never met me just wait out there in silence for me.

It might not have been those I saw and heard comment on my slave wanted sign, but instead someone who I never even noticed read the sign and then caught sight of me out the corner of their eye before they went and found someone to tell about me.

I can no more say I own my own soul, life or body than I can tell Mr. Skeeter – no, Tom says it is Mrs. Skeeter – not to have me with her tiny stick sucker to take my blood what little that may be.

"Don't you even think of moving, Boy."

"And why might I have cause to do that?" I answer.

"Don't go getting smart. I have a musket leveled right at your heart. Don't I, John?"

Funny thing is, though I can't even see my soon-to-be captors, I can smell the corn liquor and fresh pork on their breaths sure as I can feel the growing, gnawing pain of hungering for some of what they just feasted on inside my gut – along with some fresh, warm cornbread. "A musket ain't no way to welcome a free man what is searching for work into your town. Now is that the truth?"

"I don't even want to see your papers. Leave that for the constable and sheriff to do. And I doubt very much them papers you speak of even amount to much. You look far too much like the one that's described in the signs posted all about not to be that runaway slave."

I hear hounds out back behind this cage of a space they've got me in. But they cannot keep the sound of the wren from announcing his freedom to me. Teakettle. Teakettle. Teakettle!

"Here's some breakfast for you." A red-haired man with a beard that appears in sure need of scissors slides a wood plate beneath the bars. I feel for my papers. "Do you want to see my papers yet?"

"Those papers ain't gonna mean a thing. OK. Here, give them to me – "

"No. I would just as soon wait until the sheriff comes back."

"Suit yourself. I don't care one way or the other. As I said, if you be a free black man, why you so damned starved-looking?"

I do not have an answer for him and my cleaning off the plate and sliding it back beneath the bars with clear hope for more does not do much to argue against his point. He fills the plate with more eggs and cornbread and adds a coffee tin without saying more. I do not miss seeing his face when I look up and see he is gone.

A mocker bird just outside my window – a window so small there aren't even bars on it – lights on a rake end leaning up against the building. He tightens the his feathers around his trim frame before cocking his tail in jerks more abrupt than an ax splitting kindling. "I call you mocker because you mock everything that is me with everything that is you. Right now I wish Gray were here to grab you and give you a taste of what it means to be me."

The words rise in my throat and mouth hateful, vengeful and bitter as soured milk. I do not rightly know where they just came from.

Chapter Forty-Two

"All right, let us see those papers of yours."

I hear the man's words as part of some strange dream I just had. But the clang of the iron bars being opened erases all sense of a dream. Iron is real. "They are right here, Sheriff."

"Worse for wear." The sheriff squints up his face in a quizzical sort of disgust. "Whoever you had write these for you had some laughs. 'These be papers what prove this man as to be a free man'...and 'Wilson Doodle'? What sort of name is that?"

I feel my face flush. Had I a looking glass I would surely look altered, thank you, Tom, for that word. Hell – not altered, completely changed.

"What do you say we take a short trip to the President's new mansion? Not that far a trip and then a pleasant ferry boat ride across the Potomac River as well. You're going to get to see the Potomac River. Ever seen the Potomac River?"

I want to shout to the heavens. I speak to my own cat, Gray, in a less patronizing manner. Do I look like a cat or dog? As far as you are concerned, Master Sheriff, a dog has more brains. But I ask you, has your dog ever escaped, ever had any reason for escaping from you?

Chapter Forty-Three

Mulberry Row is better kept than this place scattered up from the marshy shores of the River Potomac. Hammering fills the air surrounding me.

Dogs go on and on barking down in some low spots where some of the shacks could be slave huts. But then I see white folks in the doorways.

"He ain't going anywhere with those shackles on his wrists," says one man looking over to the sheriff who felt the need to drag me into this God-forsaken mud hole.

The house they say the President lives in is up just ahead. Looks like it actually may be in the middle of a pond but then I see it is on a bit of a rise and the swampy marsh all around it is no doubt just a bunch of water from the late rain. I hear the sound before I spy its source. My best friend the goldfinch bubbles over with sound and then I see it, up and down, fluttering up in a burst of energy, then dropping just as suddenly as if to tease the whole ground-shackled world as he bursts across an open field bright green with young corn stalks sprouting just near the edge of the President's house. Freedom. That sound defines the tiny creature and the fetters on my wrist are gone when the twitters of the goldfinch get in my heart right now.

"What are you smiling about?" asks the sheriff's boy.

I do not have to answer him. Who is he? What could it matter if his name be Thomas or Clarence, John, Samuel, or Anthony? What has he ever done? Ever made single damned nail in your life, Boy? I restrain myself from screaming as much to him at the top of my lungs and then add, and not get anything but the realization that you're gonna do the exact same thing tomorrow and the next day and the day after that yet. And all of this is without so much as a smile for the work or a thank you.

Chapter Forty-Four

"I don't think the President will take kindly to you smiling, his property gone off and left without needed work," says the sheriff. "I heard you made him the most nails of all. They need those nails. That hammering you hear has go to be going on and they got to hammer on something."

The house smells raw and smoky, as if the window cannot open and let out the bad air. Men who certainly are slaves scurry all about the floors carrying materials, wood planks, paint – and yes – nails, bucket upon bucket filled to the top with them.

"Here he is, Mr. President."

"Thank you, Sir."

"I do not know what come over me, Massa Jeff. I won't ever do it no more, ever again." The words free hollow and ridiculous in my throat and mouth. But everything from the past week comes to my eyes and I cannot see for the tears.

"You can leave us, Constable."

"Sheriff, Sir and he is a strapping fellow, Sir, a danger to us and a risk carrying him in. I truly expected something for our efforts."

Massa Jeff rubs his own hands together as if to create some needed warmth. He turns to look out the new, curtain-less glass windows while blazing sunlight pours into the room. "Get those fetters off him. He produces more nails than anyone in my family at Monticello ever has made – more than five men or boys combined."

I close my eyes as the shackles are unlocked from my feet and hands. Is that a goldfinch outside the windows, windows unfinished and rough enough that a thick book is on the sill holding the window open, one of his books?

"He needs to be beaten into submission, Sir." The sheriff walks from the room as he states his advice back at the President. "I am in Fairfax should you choose to pay me for my services."

"You will be paid, Sir." Massa Jeff's words sound lifeless and hard, not too distant from the sound of one of the nuthatch birds that creep down a hickory tree – nearly as much as they decide to go back up the shaggy trunk.

"Forgive me, Sir!" I am able to go to my knees at last. "Take me back and whip me, beat me. I am ready to be baptized and find the Lord's commands, His guidance in all. Forgiveness is all I have right now." The last words can barely rise from out of my throat and mouth. A thickening darkens them, makes them barely audible.

"Get up, James. Jamie, I just don't understand this. That is all I have to say. I am a very busy man and this is why you are so important to me."

The words sound lifeless, airless and final, words someone says when they do not have anything else to say. A breeze from outside fills the space in this underdone, newly-built house which I heard some call a white house as I was brought here. This feels like the opposite of white with the mud caking the lower reaches, though on second thought white is a fitting name for the color that rules all it sees, all that comes within its grasp.

I suspect the President would like to be back at his Monticello. What do I want? I see a familiar face, a man often at the main house at Little Mountain, with Jefferson, and now here. Somehow he looks off and confused or maybe that is just me. He pulls his hat on and does not look at Massa Jeff or me. But I see his hand go up to motion me out.

"Thank you, Massa Jeff. I shall do the right thing by you." But what is the right thing? A mocker bird lights on a hoe handle leaning up against the house. We walk soundlessly to the wagon which will take me back.

"You should be beaten for what you did. I don't know why the President did not whip you, have you thrashed, Jamie."

The black man's words surprise me with their abruptness. The mocker eyes me, his body tight, feathers close to his skinny form. Then it flutters smoothly up to a nearby wild plum tree as if to mock my very existence, my ability to do anything except exactly what everyone tells me to do. "He is welcome to whip me, whip me until I am dead. I deserve it. I know his nail production has dropped since I left. Lots of folks depend on the groceries that money from the sale of my nails get them. Let me think, they did not get their sugar, molasses, or cinnamon because of me, my lack of nail-making?"

He finally turns and looks me in the eyes, searching my face for something else, some answer not so simple yet beautifully logical. The mocker bird agrees. The feathery machine grabs a luckless caterpillar from the grass after scolding us from a tree. That mocker bird is as confused about me and what I did as this house servant about to carry me back to Massa Jeff's Little Mountain.

Chapter Forty-Five

Gray's as excited about getting up in the morning now as I am. I sit outside my shack and listen to the old familiar sounds as I wait for the light to form and bring form to this world I have been dragged back to.

My old cat sits for awhile with me, lets me pull the weed burrs off his hide, never even flinching as tufts of his fur rip up off his skin with each yank of a spikey seed. Afraid he has got the tapeworm like some of the children get. He is all bone and fur on a scrawny tough hide.

Rain patters on my face all of a sudden and I go into my shack. Gray slips in at my feet, jumping up on the table and licking at the butter. Whatever he's got inside his hide – tapeworm maybe – I do not want. I toss him out the door. He never seems to mind this or complain in the least, just shakes himself and walks off as if nothing unusual just happened.

"Got some biscuits if you want them, Jamie. Just out of the fire at my place. Taking them to the boys what – "

"I know all 'bout the boys and them starting into their work, Wilson." I slam the door to give him a final answer on what I think of his biscuits and him, his whole sorry self.

"Suit yourself, Jamie. Just out of the oven. Drip some of that fresh butter and honey of yours on them."

"Go to hell, Wilson." I did not mean for the words to slip out. But now that they have, it feels just fine. I do not hear anything from his lips now, whereas I was certain I would have heard more had I not said as much. He does not go on about me having to work in the main nail shed for a time, something we both know, but he seems to want to talk about it far too much. "Those freedman papers did not say much about me being a free man." I shout the words after him out the doorway and instantly regret saying as much. "Be different next time, Master Wilson. I do not consider you nothing, not least of which a friend of any sort."

Chapter Forty-Six

"Why can't you make as much as Jamie here?" Wilson's father, Gabriel Lily, digs his fingers into the back of a little boy I heard him call Daniel. Daniel's eyes are sunk far into his face far more than they should be on a boy that could not be much more than eleven years.

A red bird screams his call right outside the nail shed, making my head hurt as much as it does listening to Wilson's father the slave-driver, the overseer the President feels can do no wrong. Could they read my thoughts right now they would take me out and whip me, for certain. "There. I made ten times the amount of nails this little Dan could make in a day. Let the boy go rest for a change."

"Maybe better if you don't come down here to the main nail shed and that you stick to your own place by yourself. You know it don't work that way. How's this new boy, Daniel, ever going to get good at this with listening to that?" Red bird has gone quiet or flown off. I picture he is insulted by Mr. Overseer's words.

In the late morning, after working for some six or seven hours by candlelight for Lord's sake, I head back to my place. I start up the fire there and commence chopping wood.

I like chopping wood, easy work that could go on and on as you can never have enough firewood to feed the oven to create the precious charcoal for burning, no matter what.

"Surprised, really surprised to see you back here, Jamie." Wilson speaks from the doorway, more out than in.

"I do not think I want to talk to you, Sir." I sputter out the words wishing I was that handsome blue jay on the ground just yonder and the acorn he was pecking could be your head, Wilson.

"Not sure why you be treating me this way. What did I do?"

"What did you do? What did you have in them manumission papers you writ for –"

"Can't help how people interpret things I write. I cannot control that. I did my best."

"You did your best?" I smack a piece of kindling wood so hard that it splits the base stump below.

"Looks like you better get another splitting log, Jamie."

We both stand staring at the log, useless now on the ground. I want to tell him I will do it right the next time. I will not use his services to help with my papers. I want to say as much just to see the shock on his face, to control him as his father controls the young lives that he has in his hands. Only they are not lives. They are equipment for making nails. Nails. Nails. Nails. "Nails!"

"What?"

"You got enough nails today? No, your pa got enough nails?" I smile, broad and open.

Wilson screws up his face and wonder of wonders, smiles back at me. Then I smile to myself. I controlled you, white man. Just taught myself a lesson with that.

"Young boy, Daniel, is doubly lucky."

"Why is that, Wilson?"

"The President's decreed that we all have tomorrow off for the Independence Day holiday celebrations. The Fourth of July just happens to be young Daniel's birthday too."

"Lucky boy. Lucky us. We all shall be celebrating Independence Day together. I would say that be as right as this rain starting to get even harder now. Come in and have a cup of coffee with me. We can celebrate on the third of July too. Independence. Would that be the same thing as freedom, Mr. Wilson?"

Chapter Forty-Seven

The door to the metal rod supply shed was left unlocked again and after such a short time of my getting back, no one seems even to take note that my leaving was not a trip see the President at his asking. I left this place. I did something I was not told to do.

A flycatcher with his funny crest-like head is wheep-wheeping up at the top of the locust trees with their sets of many little leaves, thorny twigs and branches. He found him a nest for his family. This would surely be nice to do, that is, to go out and settle yourself and your family somewhere.

Gray found himself a friend he could make a family with. But she is too old for making little kittens. Gray is on my bad side right now. He killed him a whole family of little ones of the favorite of mine, the jewel of black and yellow, the goldfinch. Guess that act of his perhaps matches my disasters of late, my escape and being free, joyful like Mr. Goldfinch only to be crushed by Mr. Wilson's poor writing. Or was it poor for a reason? Speak of that devil – Wilson.

"What did you think of those fireworks last night, Jamie?"

"I think they kept me from getting my sleep and I am dragging this –"

"That's all the nails you made today?" Pa be getting on me if I carry a bucket that empty over to him."

"Maybe your damned pa be whipping you 'cause he knows you stole some of those nails what I, the best nail maker in the whole state of Virginia, produced."

"You're just full of yourself, Mr. Jamie. Independence Day celebration must of gone to your thick head."

Wilson is not of a mind to take too much more this morning. He grabs the bucket reluctantly, refusing to look in my eyes. I feel strong, empowered for once and in control of the situation even if it is only this brief encounter here this morning. He plods back over to Mulberry Row, getting lost among the other folks over there and the wheelbarrows moving all about. Pipes being hammered for something or other and nailing with hammers on my nails no doubt goes on in a din to make one lose their mind.

I look in both directions on the little inconspicuous path I made out beyond my shed.

Smoke rises nicely from the chimney telling all I am busy with work inside, busy until Wilson's devil pa comes to beat me for not outputting more of his damned – no – the President's damned nails.

Here. The path ends just below a hump sort of fashioned of rock and earth. I scrape away the leaves and earth to a board some four inches below the ground. Carefully, I lift it up and my bucket full of nails, my work, my money, my reward – saving for escape number two lies hidden. Let them think they know my movements my mind, me like a hand perfectly fit with a glove. But who would think of this?

Why, Tom, you would not even suspect your old friend James of something so conniving. Yes, friend, I remember that word you taught me. Always liked that one, Tom. That and several others, justification and redemption.

Chapter Forty-Eight

"You forgot to leave it open again, Jamie."

"Again? Since when have I ever left the lid on the the nail bucket in the middle of nail-making, Wilson?"

"From the looks of this floor, quite a few times."

I just want Wilson to go away, go away and leave me to my thoughts. Yes, the nails I have thrown over toward the bucket so far have hit the lid and scattered on the floor and it is too dark to see whether there is even a lid on the bucket this morning. But he has no clue why the rest of those nails would be scattered all about, or does he?

"Getting too hot in here already, Jamie. I'll leave you be. When your eyes get that set to them I know you ain't wanting no one around."

"Just tell your pa he'll have his damned quota for the day."

"I'll leave out the swearing."

I want to tell Wilson to leave it in but think better of that idea. No one has answered my question yet about getting back into town for supplies and that I take to be a good sign. They are all coming near to trusting me once more.

I look up from hammering and cutting to see Wilson has lived his word for once and taken himself out of here while I was lost in my thoughts.

Peter, peter, peter bird sounds like he laughs at my plans, as if he reads my mind. A woodpecker laughs out even louder while it sounds as if the crested flycatcher weeps and weeps for dear life.

"Hello, Master James!"

"Hello, Timothy."

"We all depending on you, you know."

I take a greasy cloth and wipe the sweat from my forehead and neck. The cloth reeks of ancient pungent sweat from God knows how many weeks' and months' time. Timothy works in the main house and gets down here from time to time when word of something special being cooked gets out. From the look of his pot, gingerly balanced on his head as he starts for the main house, some of those guests up there who hardly know we are down here slaving away, are getting a tasty treat.

"Good to be needed, I suppose, Timothy. Be even better if I had a choice about it. Then I would be appreciated."

"Where'd you learn some big word like that?"

"You remember young Tom, the one that got sent away? He told me all kinds of words."

"Tried not to listen to his rambling too much."

"You missed out, Timothy."

Chapter Forty-Nine

The sun is hot on my feet as the wagon rumbles into the village. That makes the first time since they brought me back. I think the mosquitoes have missed me the most, of anyone here, in the short time I have been gone.

"How do ye, Master Jamie?" Amos, the slave who supervises all the crop work at Massa Jeff's plantation pauses. I see from his saddle bags he has got sacks with enough seed to last for some time.

"Who you calling 'Master,' Amos? I ain't no master, Master Amos." Not sure where my words just came from. But I soon feel sheepish in saying them as I did.

"I heard you decided to take some time off, Jamie...Master Jamie. The masters be the ones what do as such, heading down to New Bern, Wilmington, or Charleston when the weather gets too frosty up here in Charlottesville or anywhere else in these old mountains."

"Never got to see no Charleston or New Bern – inside of a jail in Fairfax about all and before that the President's House in Washington City."

"Need to get someone to learn you some places, how to get there and – "

"Geography, Amos."

"Lemme guess, one of Tom's words."

I nod. But I can see Amos has had his say. He eyes a mosquito trying to find a spot on his bare arm and smacks it with his open palm. Amos looks up at me and slowly shakes his head. "Just be grateful, thankful for all of this."

I hear his horse pass and note that he has ended any debate or comments. "Oh, I am grateful, most thankful, Master Amos."

I turn to stare at his back for a brief moment. His hand goes up and tugs at his beaver felt hat in acknowledgment. I grab him and pull him down from his old horse, in my mind and demand of him just why I should be so glad, so appreciative.

Robin red breast sings his fairly monotonous song as I ride along with the wagon. A mocker bird makes me forget he is who he is. I close my eyes and hear sparrows, jay birds, red-tail hawks and yes, robins, too, all streaming out from his beaky sharp mouth. Wish I could stand up there in a tree and parrot all those people who tell me how good I've got it. I would sing a new song though, one that says I am grateful all right, grateful, well nigh thankful I've got a heart that beats free – always will, God damn it, till something or somebody stops it.

Chapter Fifty

"Good to see you again, Jamie. Missed you," says the man at the supply shed.

I want to tell him to stop. Do not make something big of my being gone no – any – more. I am back now. Please don't make it feel worse by going on about it. I smell sweet potatoes burning somewhere and it makes my stomach turn a bit.

"Some coffee for you?"

"No. Well, all right. I will –"

"No milk for it today, pretty strong, too, and that might make you jittery, although you're the last person I could imagine being jittery."

"I will take that coffee you offered me now. Got everything I need loaded up, it looks like." I do not add that he is the jittery one, in my opinion. He makes me want to jump out of my skin just listening to him with his yellow teeth he keeps flashing at me.

The coffee is tolerably good. Goes down easy despite being milk – or cream – less. I notice he has a cat that could be Gray's twin. She comes over and sits under my chair just like Gray is of a mind to do sometimes.

"You know Virginia's just passed a law what gives

free blacks just one year before they have to leave the state?" His words seem to shrink the smile, his teeth right from his face.

"I never knew that – did not really know the fact. May just explain why I don't hear from my friend, Tom Woodson much anymore."

"Well, any blacks wandering about without no master, they gonna be – what you call it? – some kind of open target for those slave catchers."

"Really." I do not really want to hear any more of his talk. I want this conversation ended. It brings me melancholy, as Tom would say from time to time, parroting his father's words.

"I heard of one poor man, he be a man, a free black, not a slave, and he was captured and the man that captured him tried to make him his slave. The free man put up a fight, was stabbed and died. And there wasn't any bringing the man what did the crime to trial. He got away with murder as far as I'm concerned."

"It was good talking to you," I lie. "Thank you, Sir, for the coffee." I keep moving, get into the wagon and start away from the platform.

Tea kettle. Tea kettle. Tea kettle of the Carolina wren sounds more urgent and of a warning now on the slow ride back. I barely touch the horse. She just goes, knows the way home.

Blackbirds with their clacking clucks loud and annoying match my mood, while the Redwing blackbird along the pond and creekside tries to counter with his konk-ko-ree. I just do not want to think about what that man told me so breezily like he was telling me one of his chickens laid an egg that was too painfully large to lay and when he cracked the thing open there were two yolks inside.

How the hell can someone such as me, who does not want this life and that will do anything to be a real man, a human man, not a slave, hog or a hammer in other words a thing, possibly get across the state of Virginia to freedom? Much as I love Virginia, it is not a good place for black folks. The same flies and mosquitoes buzz and bite those white folks who own us. Why should they be any different just because they have a paper with some stupid words – a law – written on it?

Chapter Fifty-One

"No, Miss Betty, I don't know why my cat is always getting into your food over there."

Tom's grandma, Betty Hemings stands with her fists on her hips. "I know why, James."

"Why is that?"

"You don't feed him over here. Tell me you ain't got extra cash given to you from all those nails, all those trips of yours into town."

"I really don't have any, Miss Betty," I lie. But Betty Hemings hasn't time, it appears, to argue anymore. Funny thing is I do not see Gray around anywhere. But I do see one of her tiger stripes wandering around the clover, tail straight up to the sky. "Hallo, Wilson. I said Hallo, Wilson..." No answer. I am just trying to be friendly but evidently I have said or done something to upset Mr. Wilson.

You done something to upset me. I want to shout that to him to even up the score. I see his face peeking in at me after a while though, until he walks off.

I pound the nails hard but not hard enough that I shatter them and fell the years of useless – at least for me – work craft with the strength of my knowing muscles.

Virginia law says if my mama is a black and my Pa's white I am the property of my father. The son? Not in the law's eyes. Tom used to tell me that from time to time. Funny thing is Tom's pa is now the President of this new country, and he does not seem to have any interest in his property – or his son – Tom, now Tom Woodson.

I look out into the cloudy, dreary summer afternoon. The poundings from the other nail shed go on in somewhat spastic fashion. I know new boys labor over at the other shed, doing their over-exuberant and more carelees than not, hammering.

Up I get with my kerchief and mop my temples and hair of the dripping sweat my body has found a need to create. I take a deep breath and carefully scoop up the loose nails scattered at the base of my table. Then I toss the thin iron pieces near the doors and windows, mixing them amid leaves and pine needles on the ground to let their minds wander from what is really there.

The privy is a welcome sight as I head down the trail. But none would look after a slaving heading to the privy, let alone a white man heading there. Another deep breath of the moist Virginia air and I reach the spot I have come to for a long, long time. I easily move the flat gray rocks just enough so that the leaves keep on looking like they were just blown down from the trees.

The hole is narrow and small; it is just large enough to fit my balled up fist in and my arm. I got to lie down on the ground completely to reach my hand up in there and feel the stash of nails that has ben building up a long, long while. "Hello, Freedom!" The words fly out before I can capture them, a mocker bird flying up and away from the clutches of a smooth dry black rat snake.

"Who you talking to, Jamie?" Wilson is far enough away that I have time to pull my arm out and recap the spot. "Looked to me like you be laying on the ground. What you be doing that for?"

"You ain't needing to be asking as I told you all about that before, Wilson."

"And what that be, Jamie?"

"You ever made a single nail in your life?"

"Why'd I do something foolish like that. That's what you're for."

I ignore his cruelty, one he has not a clue about. "I am a tall man. Years of stooping over that fire hunching down and even though I be a young man, I still got to stretch out from time to time. Ground's as good a place as any else for doing that."

"What about them rocks there?"

"I try not to lie on rocks. Now if you would be so kind, I go some work to finish up." I motion toward the privy and Wilson shakes his head at my shallow joke.

I hear his steps heading up the trail and out of earshot.

Chapter Fifty-Two

The sack of nails is heavy on my back. With one hand I pat my pocket to feel the manumission papers resting there and with the other hand as I switch the hands carrying the sack, I feel for the money – coins – in my other pockets. Pants with pockets. I earned these for my hard work. What did they think a slave would use pockets for anyways? It is as if they do not think at all. Well, property doesn't think – or does it?

The breeze, strong and hot makes lots of sound in the trees all around. But above all of that comes the sound of the bells from churches down the way along the river. The though comes to me that red pepper – cayenne is also in a sack inside the nail bag. I must remember to take that out before I sell the nails. Painful as the stuff is inside my shoes, the bloodhounds hate it worse. Yesterday I recalled Tom telling me that information – another one of his words – long ago. Of course that was long before I got the idea in my brain that running off could be a good thing, that I could do this if I wanted to.

All along the wharf people swarm. But there is not anyplace to go along the river except for two ways. Behind me a steep bank, mostly red broken bricks forms something of a wall. While to each side people move with sacks of grain, wheelbarrows filled with firewood, bundles of sticks, baskets of bread, loads of lumber – this last makes me smile. One cannot do anything with lumber unless you have my nails to put it all together. Wood pegs are used too, but as Tom told me, iron nails used in lumber mean more prestige for the builder.

I see a shed down the way. "You needing nails to sell?"

The man looks up as soon as my words escape my lips. "Always looking for nails to sell. You must have seen all that loose lumber out there. Lots to be built."

I like the way his eyes do not linger on my face, as

if he has more important things to do than figure me out. No questions about my being a free man or what master I bring these nails down here to the river for.

"What do you have?"

I set the sack on the bench beside his table so as not to draw attention to it had I set it up on the main table.

"My God!"

Again the clang of nearby church bells shroud the events unfolding. I let out a breath. A dog barks stupidly just outside the door followed by a yelp. "Shut your mouth, mongrel." Another yelp.

"What are you asking?"

"I usually get 50 and –"

"I was going to offer you 100. Which do you prefer, 50 or 100?"

"Fifty would be fine," I reply, stupidly, thinking instead of the senseless punished bark of the mongrel dog. Now I simply want to be away from this place more than anything.

"Suit yourself then. Enjoyed doing business with you, Mister..."

"Woodson, Gerald Woodson."

"Mr. Gerald Woodson. Come back, or you can send your slave."

I fight to get a normal breath out at these last words. The dog barks its comical annoying bark, crying out before I hear the stick smashing its back. I reach up and pull on the edge of my hat and walk out into the river of bodies along the waterfront, jealous of the silent brooding – free – stream of eddying currents and muddy, wild, rain-fed water none here dare plunge into. But then I look out to the big houses just up the hill with their chimneys and birds that could be flying free, well as a bird can be, yet having to plunge down within the red chimneys to make their way to their homes.

And I wish I had a home, not someplace where I was forced to stay like at the little mountain of the President, but a place out on the bushes amid the brushy chokecherry trees where I could hear the old "Sam Peabody, Peabody, Peabody" of the white throat sparrow and –

"You're in my way. I'm trying to get up to the hanging before it's too late." The bald-headed man seems not to see me. I am just an obstruction to him. His tone of voice is the one which one might use as they are shoving a huge dresser out of the way of a window one want to peer though.

"Up this way, Hurry." A woman this time and all of a sudden I am swept along by a gently moving throng of people heading up a gradually rising street alongside the river.

The crowd thickens every so often as more people of all sizes come from alleys and down out of doorways. I peer up the cobblestone street that moves slowly away from the turbulent river and the sounds of the crowd, their excitement, murmurs, shouts, laughter and even some crying from somewhere, carry away all sounds or thoughts of this river just below us. Now we travel in a human river.

There it is. There is the reason for the excitement. I catch it from my eye's corner and it stops my heart. The fresh-built gallows appears from time to time when some short people allow me a glimpse of its hooked wood and noose.

"Why they gonna hang him, Mama?" I don't see the boy yet. But when his mother's large body shifts as soon as I can see him, he stares up into my eyes.

"It's called a capital crime when there be stealing involved. Capital means it will be a hanging."

"They are hanging someone for stealing something, Mama? Killing someone for such as that?"

"It's just a slave I heard and you know that if a slave's being hung they must have really proved worthless. That's valuable property otherwise."

"I thought property means lands."

Before she can reply, a man ahead of them answers without turning around. I hear the red bird and the Carolina wren above the din of voices for some reason as if they sound their calls to beckon us all to a better place, someplace where hanging is not part of that world. "He's no slave," I shout to no one in particular. "Been a freeman all his life. Made the mistake of helping a slave, one that has not been recovered to the rightful owner of the property."

I smell the pungent smoke of a fire with charcoal and coal burning and hear the stead clang of a smith hammer. I feel homesick for the security of the nail shed, the absolute certainty of it. But a flock of blackbirds cackling overhead and the din of mocker birds makes me let that thought pass. You cannot long for the uncertainty of a life that is not yours.

"That man talks about people as property too, Mama."

"Not people, Nate. Slaves." Her words spill out quicker than any blackbird warning clucks.

"Said slave, you assisted in the theft and then subsequently stole three sacks of flour and two sacks of sugar..." announces the man directing this event.

"I told you stealing was a capital offense."

"But Mama, the man said he is a free man."

The man turns and looks down, then replies in a level voice. "Ma'am, may I explain to him?"

She motions with her chin and smiles.

"If a slave steals, this means death if he is caught son. If not caught any who assisted him must pay with their – "

"If I had helped the slave would I hang?" The boy's question catches the two adults towering over him by surprise.

"No." The mother blurts her reply and turns toward the gallows as if she would prefer not to hear from anyone else on this matter.

"Of course you, as a white would not hang. But you may be in for a fine or a trip to jail," adds the man, quietly.

"That's not fair. That's a freeman they are hanging, with the same rights as – "

"Not quite true, Son."

"I am not your son."

A long murmur arises from the crowd, then silence except for the steadily creaking pine timbers as the body rocks back and forth.

Chapter Fifty-Three

My own mind starts to wander and rock like the breeze whipping the tulip tree branches just before a storm would crash at Little Mountain, Monticello. Why such a hold on me? When I am at that place I own nothing, not even myself.

They can give me coins, shoes or shirts as well as breeches but being that I do not own myself how could anything that is by me be truly owned? Wren's teakettle – teakettle – teakettle sounds bright and alive. They help me to get the vision of what I have just seen from out of my head. A spider bites the back of my ankle. I know that feeling sure as I know my own fingernails. It is like the pain in the mind not there one moment and then, without even feeling the tiny creature crawling about on the skin, pain is there like a painful memory. I know where I must go.

The aimlessness of this time draws me to my folks. I know I am doomed, somehow know it to be a matter of time before the knock comes to the door. I inquire on the direction of Poplar Forest Plantation, asked one group which way it be, hinting that the reason I must go there would be to going up with my work gang. A black man on a road heading to other black men enslaved and working their backs off makes perfect sense.

Flies buzz about my feet and now the wren makes a much more urgent call than ones I heard along the river as if he is warning me off from here. Mr. Bluejay hopped up into the pecan branches in silence as if he is one of Massa Jeff's trackers spying on me. "I am not afraid of you, Mr. Jay. Go on and sick your hounds on me. Their bites be bigger than this spider bite. But pain is still pain."

Chapter Fifty-Four

Low mumbles from the cabins mean there isn't anyone moving out of their doors anytime soon. Sun's been down at least an hour and now that bellies are full of cornbread, back or pork and maybe some turnip greens, sleep will be these folks' recreation until the bell sounds hours before dawn. And thank you, Tom. I remembered what recreation means. Do black folks ever in their lives have recreation? Is singing while weeding tobacco fields recreation?

"Anyone home?" The question feels beyond silly. I knock again. Low mumbling provides me with an answer. "Mama? Pa?"

"Jamie? Is that you, Boy?"

I cannot say if it is just that Pa is worn out or half asleep. But his voice clearly has lost some of its power, like a flag with those infernal stars and stripes laying close against a flagpole instead of flapping hard in the breeze.

I smell the familiar vaguely spicy smell of their bodies. Ma still snores. Not like her to – "Ma? Mama, why don't you – "

"That's not your Mama, Son." Pa's words sound much more clear and focused now.

"But – "

"Your mama died two – no – three years back."

"Where's Gray, Jamie?" At least my sister is still here I think to myself. I distance myself without even realizing it, from the woman sleeping where my mother had slept all my young life.

"She caught the milk sick, son. Didn't last long at all. Helen is a good woman. Wish you could know her."

I sit in my old stool in the corner, half expecting Gray to rub on my ankles at any time. Instead I just feel tiny mosquitoes flying up my pant cuffs, shirt sleeves as well as around my neck and chest to bite hard, painful. I smack the places, noting none of my old family appears so afflicted by them.

"They be tired out from our blood, Son. Guess they be wating some fresh healthy blood." Pa always could read my mind. I hear a senseless bark from out behind the shed and wonder if it is part of a pack of dogs getting ready to hound me. I hear tolling bells far off. The sound seems to go on forever, like this time, this journey of mine to stay free, escaped. Out beyond the doorway I spy a cat chewing on something. This light almost makes it look like it is Gray. The creature catches my eye and walks my way.

"That one could be a brother of Gray, Jamie," whispers Mary, my sister.

"Don't get him talking. He needs to go." Pa's words hurt even if they are true. Cannot remember how long the huggings lasted but not as long by any means as I would have liked them to.

The sun is nearly up now. Some kind of light gives form to the trees. A woodpecker sounds as if he is ready to peck my neck, so close by as he is.

I know this place. I look for the little path as I remember it but the trees in the years I have been gone now have thickened and made the trail nearly indistinguishable from the rest of the forest floor. My voice chokes in my throat.

Time. I feel the weight of time in these trees, mere saplings when I left, now thickening into maturity and old age. Here time has actual weight, startling to me. None see this except me – somebody who has been away from this place.

I hear trouble now. Baying hounds getting closer may mean they suspected I would come back home after all. I shut my eyes and pray the prayer of the fearful, the condemned and know that sometimes it only works to start over, all over once more.

"Haven't gotten word back yet on how much of a whipping you should get, Jamie." Gabriel Lilly for all the fear he instilled in me over the years, looks shrunken somehow, less of a man, less of anything, the skin of a boiled sweet potato without much meat left within, brimming to get beyond the dark husk.

"Just call me 'James'. I ain't Jamie no more. That be a little boy's name – "

"I guess I'll be calling you whatever I want, Jamie."

"Suit your own damned self." I am not of a mind to talk to Gabriel Lilly nor his mealy-mouthed son Wilson at the moment. The air is sticky. This fire makes things hotter but it drives away the moisture – and the damned skeeters. Clink. Clink. Clink! The hammer's blow seems to vanquish Lilly's face from my sight. This act of mine in my mind softens his hard angular edge and the wrinkles starting to crease his worn out face. A few more bangs and I can tell the sound, smoke and heat will drive he and Wilson back out into the sure embrace of the mosquitoes.

This spring and summer have been the wettest any can recall and the mosquitoes have exploded into the air with a vengeance. Teacher. Teacher. Tea kettle! The wren is gonna have to do more than just sing to get these skeeters in check.

"How long you been wearing those leg irons?" I hear the voice despite my hammerings. I quit the strokes and stop pumping the bellows which already has the fire to near to blue-hot with heat and flames.

The man must stoop to come through the doorway. His frame is angular and tall, newly muscled but its shape immediately suggests Massa Jeff for some reason. But this ain't the President – for certain.

"You gonna ask me in, Jamie? Starting to rain again outside here."

"They don't call me Jamie no more."

"Any more, James." Tom comes in and holds my hands out toward the light of the doorway. He shakes his head as he runs his fingers over the scars and cracks, studying them as if they hold the clues to all of the secrets of Monticello, if not the whole entire universe. "Ain't no universe here at this place," he whispers reading my thoughts as only Tom can.

"You always could know what I am thinking, on the the spot."

"Massa Jeff creates his fake, false universe with slaves what – no – that cannot ever be seen. But instead they scurry beneath the house like moles or weasels pursing the moles, all to feed the unknowing, unaware, unfeeling ridiculous white folks above. Can't say I blame you for running off. You got to get better, though, Jamie, sorry, James."

I fight to contain my feelings, try my hardest. I concentrate on the buzzing of something hovering about my face in the gloom of this space. When I stay still, the leg irons feel nearly as if they're not there. Slightest twist or move though and their weight makes me want to shout out at the top of my voice to strip them off from my ankles. I focus on some demanding baby bird I hear just outside the shed with its pleading high-pitched and endless. Could it be a baby cowbird three times the size of some warbler or sparrow working the foster mother half to death to fill its stomach? Greedy thing. Greedy like these whites that take all from us and think that that be just fine because, well they're smarter and better at reading and ciphering – and we are just dark black animals after all and to chain us up and sell us like horses or hogs in the market makes it so. Don't you –

"James! James, I have been talking to you. Are you listening? Do you even hear me?"

"Yes. I hear you, Tom."

"Then what have I just told you?"

I look down at the leg irons. Tom kneels and fingers them while slowly shaking his head. His eyes catch mine and we stare into each others faces melting the years away. All at once he's the little boy and I am the one who always watched out for him, guiding him despite the fact that he had all the privileges, despite the fact that he was the son of a black mother – even if barely black at that – and a white father making him forever the property of that father, one who even gave him his name. Yet Tom was sent away, given another name, Woodson and freed at least in actuality if not word heritage.

"Can't stay long. Everyone gets nervous when I am around and those leg irons look tempting to someone who would just as soon claim I ain't free but their property as they slapped them on my skinny ankles."

Tom takes a long, deep breath. The blessed, sweet cooling breeze outside echoes his sound. We both sit and drink it in like the honeysuckle nectar we sucked from the little white flowers as boys. "Next time – be there a next time – head west," whispers Tom, more an inward breath than even a whisper, a distant owl call in the night you are not even sure was real. His eyes drop to the chain and leg irons. "And I will get you something for that."

We move among the charcoal ovens as if in a dream. Only sounds at times are the clinks of my ankle chains. The smell of the cone-shaped ovens tells us both, more than the temperature that the precious wood, now compressed into even more useful charcoal for keeping the smithing fires burning, is done and ready. He grabs a bigger stack than I after I unshovel the stuff and we pile the pieces in each others arms to carry the short distance to the nail shed. No ones eyes bother to catch ours as we do our work for a few trips, none that is until the clear clinks of my irons draw eyes to my feet somehow magnetically. Then, a darkness comes to the faces. As if a freshly built spider web in a dark corner had just been discovered.

Chapter Fifty-Five

Some other cat – not Gray – has taken to hanging around the shed. His meowing is nothing like Gray's and it does a good job of hiding the sound of my leg iron clinking when I move.

Tom did come through and sent me a file and a metal cutter blade that I keep hidden under the front door jam for safe keeping. Every morning before anyone notices that I ought to be at work I rub some licks out of the irons. They grow thinner and thinner with each passing day. But they still manage to stay on my ankles miraculously enough so all think it's well with me and my further limbs enslavement.

"The irons must be starting to bother you by about now," says Wilson. He stands in the doorway right above the place where I hide my file and metal saw. He's even friends with the little man what snuck them up to me, nodding when I mentioned Tom Woodson's name.

"Worse when a mosquito gets behind the metal and bites just where I ain't able to scratch, Wilson."

"I imagine that would be irritating."

"You probably could not imagine. Have you ever worn leg irons?"

"What do you think, Jamie?" His question dangles and floats like the skeeters trying to find some place to land on me or Wilson in order to get themselves a meal of fresh blood.

"So what are you going to do today?" The question seems to take us both by surprise. I am uncertain as to why I asked it and Wilson screws up his face as if it will take some time to answer it. Wren screams out some bird frustration matching the mood in here at the moment.

"Starting to rain without again," Wilson goes on. "Not much to do when that happens." He moves out form the doorway and into my shed. He can do me no more wrong. I have gotten over what he did with the manumission papers which he wrote up for me and that lost me my first freedom, my first real escape.

The cat starts in with his mournful crying as if to emphasize my feelings of when I saw Wilson's written words done me worst than any good, got me captured and enslaved once more. The clinking of the ankle irons lets me realized that the second time it was my own tender family feelings what trapped me. "Next time it be different."

"What do you mean, Jamie?"

"Next time that tiny wren calls he would sound so angry." The brown bird calls his tea kettles to confirm my words and get me out of trouble. "Watch out for that rangy cat Mr. Wren. He be angry hungry and sounds a mess today."

Chapter Fifty-Six

I grab the cornbread from out of the warming pot and the lump of butter someone's dripped on the top of the chunks lets me forget about the metal at my ankle once more. I shift position and it all comes back to me again.

People keep in motion, bringing pots of cabbage and sweet potatoes, okra stewed and slimy yet wondrous. The gloppy mess of it overflowing as it is lugged up to the main house. Massa Jeff likes to tell visitors that us slaves could not live without the food he supplies us. Truth is he could not live without all the food we grow in our gardens and he buys back for pennies. Truth is we'd be dead if we tried to leave on those slim pickings he calls food that he leaves for us.

There are lots of carriages I see from this angle, means there are lots of hungry people wanting this herb-broiled fresh pork, chicken legs, ham hocks, turkey breasts and biscuits not to forget peaches and its cobbler, raspberries and apple fritters working their way up to the house, big-domed and setting their like an overdone, over-stuffed pig or turkey.

The folks of course, don't go through the main door, but underneath, through side doors that bring you to a place under the house. Anyone can travel in and out of that arrow straight space, like some sorta two-legged mole man. They just can't ever go up above a floor to where their existence hardly counts for anything. There they don't go in through the main door but underneath where visitors would gasp were they to see all the crazy goings-on.

An ant mound of movement gets the food up, on rope-towed lifts to rooms where the food appears as if some sorcerer did her conjurings – wand and all. But those are smart white folks – are there any other kind, according to them – who do not believe in such as that. Just what do they believe?

They are afraid of seeing some dark-skinned person – a person I say who would not be a slave. No. Slave they say as a slave ain't no person and can be owned, can be –

"James?" The voice is low and quite pretty, one I cannot recall ever hearing let alone imagining.

"That's what they tend to call me here, that or 'Jamie'. Only I don't know that I take to that one anymore and – "

She puts a finger to my lips, slowly shaking her head. The teakettles of the wren have gone quiet as has all around but for some bird needing to be fed and making an awful fuss. A tiger-striped cat sits statue-like. All at once I see Gray shuffling around and sniffing the tall weeds.

"Good you act distracted right now," she whispers, her eyes narrowing. She slides a white bundle into my hand. "See if you can figure out how to use this. Big strapping man like you should be able to do that."

I want to answer but she breaks off a piece of my cornbread from out of my hand and stuff it into her mouth to crush out the air of delicacy and intelligence about her. Were any to be watching right now they would see an ignorant slave woman, fit for spawning yet more pieces of salable equipment for this place and some sort of work only – not clever enough to do what she has just done for me.

I file slow and deliberate just before the sun fills this place with other sounds. I like it that way, like the thinning of the hard metal with time, gives me time to see how quick it is to clap some hard cold metal onto a human limb and then how it can take a lifetime in turn to get the thing off that same leg or wrist.

Gray's got to be touching me. That be with his tail or head or some part of his body as if he would die if that connection be broken.

"I heard a sound from without that sounded a bit different, Jamie. And what you doing in here so early in the morning?"

"I find the nail rod does better if it has been smoothed out a bit, Wilson," I lie.

"That's the most ridiculous thing I have ever heard." The words fly out like gnats before he can rein them in.

I shrug my shoulders and act like it is none of my business what he thinks.

Smack!

"What did you do that for, James?"

"Now, when I slap you I'm James not Jamie? You had a big old skeeter just a draining your fat cheek of all of its blood, Sir."

Wilson raises a hand to his cheek and slowly rubs. He considers me for a long moment and I hold his gaze as long as he will mine. I want to say to him, to ask him why he's looking so intently into the face of a piece of property. You would not gaze into the eyes of that mule, horse, sheep or goat out there or even into the face of Gray who sits back licking furiously at his legs and feet. His long what legs and feet make it look like he has always got on a pair of white boots, at least on his back legs –

"Well I just can't explain that sound I heard earlier and what you might have been doing in here."

I point to another mosquito starting in on her work just above his cheekbone. Want to add that thanks to Tom I can tell him it be a she not a he, but that be more evidence of thinking, remembering and –

"And don't you be going to slapping my face again."

"Sometimes, Wilson it be the only way – "

"Any slapping to be done on me, I will do it. And Gabriel is needing – "

"His quota, Massa Jeff's quota you mean. Hard to get work done when you be talking to someone."

I hear his footsteps out the door and up the path. My file works on the inside of the iron where it won't be seen right off. One, two, three, four – up to nine passes and still I hear his footsteps going off up the hill. No pauses. He did not hear this time. Neither Wilson, nor anyone else won't ever hear this sound again. I vow that. It be my sound. That noise, what a simple little sound that it makes, shall be my very own racket. This belongs to me and is the joyful sound of freedom being born yet one more time.

Chapter Fifty-Seven

The clang of bells in the village below the little mountain tells me something is burning somewhere. The ringing comes fast and quick-paced and then as if whoever rang that bell got tired out, ceases as quick as it started.

The old horse does not notice the clanging or chooses to ignore it. When it ceases, a regular old church bell starts up. Now he pauses and his ears perk up as if that was the sound he was waiting for.

"Mama, why does that man have a big bar on the bottom of his leg, one made of iron metal?" The boy walks between two other boys as their mother leads them away from the village. The boys all carry sacks of grain suited to their own sized bodies it seems.

"That's not a man, Son. That's a slave. The irons on his legs make sure he doesn't run off."

"Does he belong to the President, Mama?" The largest of the boys asks this question. He turns and looks back at me.

I narrow my eyes and hold his gaze as long as I can before sticking my tongue out as far as it will go, crossing my eyes all at the same time.

"Good question, Son. He probably does. Monticello is in the direction he comes from."

Gray nudges my feet, irritated by the irons, no repelled by them as much as I am. He paws and scratches right at the place where my file has been steadily thinning the iron.

My legs are blistered and sore where the metal will not allow for free air to reach the place, not wet sweaty air where my own body keeps to generating intervals of heat locked right around the iron.

I toss Gray into the back of the wagon amid the sacks of burlap. He comes right back to me and rubs against my legs, staring into my face as if the offending toss never happened.

"Gonna miss you, Gray." in case any mother learning her children about the difference between men and mindless slave property should sneak up as I clop along. "This time I ain't coming back. Got careless before. I won't this time. Nothing for me at home. Pa's got a new woman. She's no mother to me. Not sure how much of a wife she is to Pa."

"Who you talking to, your cat?" The man smiles up at me with a missing tooth in the middle of his mouth.

I want to ask him what he is doing listening to the words of a piece of property for. "I do that sometimes, talk out loud when no one is there. Got to get them words out quick at times."

The man is gone before I can even add to my answer. I take a deep breath. He did not notice my iron fetters or if he did he somehow knew it was none of my business what he though of them. "Why can't more be like you, Sir?"

The man does not choose to turn around or he is out of earshot. Whichever it may be shall vex me the rest of this day.

The grain and tools make the wagon groan creak under the weight. The old cart exhales its age now.

"Them irons don't look too comfortable, Jamie."

"Just shut up about them." The words slip out before I can stop them. But for some reason I resist a glance his way, do not look up to see Dan's eyes or the effect my carelessness may have had on him. Finally I raise my face and gaze over at his.

"Just making small talk, Jamie. Didn't mean to upset you. Not like you need to be reminded that you have them on. Looks like they don't do very well by your ankles."

I want to tell him everything I can about them, spill my thoughts and let them drone on like the cicadas and their intonation in the treetops, the incessant trill of the wren before it finally teakettles its calls or the catbird spewing on with his chattering most un-catlike warning. The handsome gray bird's meow sounds falser than a child attempting the sound for the very first time. Suns pours down like hot runny honey now that the rain's finally done worn itself out.

"Here. Rub some of this on it, Jamie."

"I don't know – "

"Go ahead. Don't argue, Jamie."

I take a lump of the stuff and rub it from my fingertips down around the skin that does not seem skin anymore. For once the unshakable pain from my lower legs lets my face fall just a bit and relax.

"Better?"

I nod without speaking.

"You about done out there?" His wife calls impatiently from the other side of the burlap curtain at the wooden loading platform "Oh, you," says the woman. "James you you need to take yourself and your ugly leg irons back to the nailery. You been here long enough. A long line is forming down the way too."

Dan takes a scoop of the thick lard-like stuff and plops it into a cotton sack. He fits that into another larger burlap sack and hands it to me, atop the last sack of oats I take from him.

"Did you pay for that, James?"

"Ignore her, Jamie."

"You need not be supplying Monticello's slaves with stuff, gratis, Daniel."

I slap a mosquito on my forearm and notice Dan's wife shake her head and slap her neck and arms. Then she hurries inside from the growing clouds and drizzle, back behind the burlap curtain.

Chapter Fifty-Eight

Wasps buzz in tortured cyclones about the ground looking insane to find something. The steady hacking of the ground with tools makes me feel sorry for the ground sometimes. She gives us so much, all that we eat and all that we do is hack at her.

"How are those irons feeling today, Jamie? Looks like you're getting along well with them lately."

"Are you now taking to sneaking up on people, Wilson?"

"Just making conversation with you, Jamie."

I do not know that I like his way of conversing this morning. I take a deep breath to still my racing heart. I don't want him to notice that all my filing of the ankle irons has made them nearly paper thin in some places. Aside from my being so used to them now, they are also reduced and lighter. It would be a disaster if Wilson got wind of that.

"You don't trust me, Jamie, do you?"

I drag my sack over from one row I have been working on and start in to digging a fresh row. The sweet potatoes are plentiful this year just below the damp earth. As I kneel I turn around and notice his gaze on my leg irons. I shift my body to make the ankles clang together creating the most sound possible. "Well you try living with them on your ankles always and see how quiet you can keep them."

"I wasn't saying anything."

A squirrel comes noisily down a bordering pecan tree. The flying shaggy bark and barking rodent takes both of our minds and talk off this present sour conversation.

"You like digging sweet potatoes better than making nails?"

"What kind of question is that? Does it matter what I like?" I pick up a huge sweet potato and throw it with all my might at the squirrel. For some reason the animal stays fixed to the side of the tree while the potato smashes into the trunk in an explosion of orange glop. The creature's tail starts vibrating nearly as much as its mouth chirps. "It is good to get out from the smoke and nails and the gloom of that shed from time to time, Wilson."

The whole scene and its action has taken Wilson's eyes off my leg irons and freed me from my dark humor. "Guess I just liberated that tuber – Tom told me that's what they really are – of it's skin."

Flies already buzz about the mess on the tree and ground. "Guess everything's a slave to something,

flies always got to be where there's a clean up needed just like them vultures circling up above, patiently waiting to spy them a corpse down here below."

"I ain't no slave."

I don't argue with Wilson on that point. No matter what, he is a slave too. But I remain the one who is the slave in name and treatment, hold that label more than that of the name Ma and Pa proudly gave me.

Chapter Fifty-Nine

Mosquitoes try to get some of my blood out but then rise up in frustration. These hands are thick and tough. I squish some of the little devils on my forearms as they try to have better luck than those on my hands.

The file makes its dry rasp steady and smooth now on the leg irons, one and then another. The hazy sun will be up soon. An owl sounds as if it is right outside my door. Who All! Who All! Could not sound any closer than that.

"You ain't gonna find any more of a meal than these mosquitoes will provide for you, my friend."

The metal is so thin now it could be easily bent and eventually cut off from my ankles by hand.

"What you doing up so early, Jamie?"

"And what are you doing wandering about in the dark for, Wilson?"

"Couldn't sleep."

"So you come over to nag at me?"

He does not answer me. I hear him walking around without for a time. Not thinking or maybe beyond caring, I move the file a few more steady, even strokes, back and forth – back and forth – and finally just a steady grating of metal on metal rings up from my ankles. Then the wren tea kettles over the noise with an early outburst.

"What do you know about the western part of Virginia, Wilson?" My sudden question takes even me by surprise.

"Can I come in? I hate talking to a door."

I push the door open. More light streams in as the sun is about to steal all this blessed darkness from the place.

"Gray needs to be careful with that owl about. Just heard the thing."

"I heard it too, Wilson. You come all the way over here to tell me that?" I catch his eyes and try to figure him out. They tell me nothing. I have no trust for this man. But I also have absolutely no fear of him. I can make my own way. Wilson has never had to worry about being owned by someone, someplace. "Gray's got nothing much on his bones. Owl gets him, owl gets him. Sometimes I think that owl does not bother with him because she knows bones make a poor dinner for her owlets."

"'Owlets?' You make that up? And how would you know that's a she-owl calling out there?" Wilson takes a seat on a stump beside the door. I can tell he is working on my original question. "Pa took me out to the western part of Virginia a time or two to hunt. The people out there are different."

I wait for him to give me a reason why the people might be different. Slap!

"Why'd you do that?"

"Mosquito on your neck getting a red belly full of blood."

But now Wilson's white neck is smeared with red.

"Lot of creeks out to the west – and ravines."

"What's a ravine?"

"You should know that."

"Shut your mouth, Wilson."

He motions to the other side of Monticello with his chin and then points, spreading his fingers out. "I don't think I'd like living in the west. Not much there. The owls would probably eat your cat just to be mean."

Within, I warm to the fact that Wilson did not quite see the reason I am asking about the western part of Virginia. That is news I am liking the sound of. No people. No control. Owls that maybe threaten along with other animals ready to spook the bloodhounds, and lots of creeks for those bloods to lose your scent in.

I fight the urge to smile. Managing Wilson the way he did to me on my first escape, gives me an even better feeling inside.

"You got something to do now, Wilson? I need to be about my work with the nails or tending to the charcoal fires."

Later in the afternoon the thrasher bird startles me. The thing is quiet for a change, it hardly makes a sound as it goes about scattering leaves and grass to find some grubs. "You ain't living up to your name, Thrasher-bird. But those pretty feather of yours define the color brown and – "

"Hey, Jamie who you be talking to now?"

"Just noticing how that thrasher-bird, Mama's mistress said it be cousin to the mocker-bird, goes about his work mighty quiet for some reason."

"Don't have anything to say about no birds. Just here to tell you my father's got a job for you if you be done."

I shake my head and raise a hand to cut him off. Then I pull up the bucket of nails from out the shed and shake it.

Loose nails within are so solid in the full container they barely make a sound. When I hand the bucket to Wilson I smile on the inside; he can barely lift the thing.

One of Gray's new friends, a mousy, tiger-striped, sorry excuse for a house cat, meows annoyingly as if he expects me to do something for him. That is just how I want it to be with me. Let the whites howl and meow their complaints all the while I go about my business of escaping for good, just as the silent thrasher-bird has not drawn attention to itself and lives to see another sunrise.

"Pa wants you to pick up all the tools that have

been repaired. I don't know why, but you don't even have to let him know when you're back from town."

Again, I smile inwardly. Well that hurts my soul. I cannot even tell him thank you for the job and remind him how nice this newly-fixed spade rests in my hand? I bite a green apple and savor the sourness and how it occupies my mouth so I do not need to talk to Wilson.

"No. He must trust you, somehow, at the same time he'd rather not have to think about you."

"Strange answer, Wilson. Where is the wagon I will take?" I hurry into my shed and grope beneath the mats resting on the bare ground to find my old file. When I go I will swap this old worn one for a new one. Now that smile fills my face.

"What you grinning at Jamie?"

"At how bold that thrasher-bird is this afternoon. Look. He flew up on that fence right there after butchering a cicada and feasting on it while cats are all on the prowl. Boldness can profit you at times, Wilson."

"And at times you can get yourself hung as well, Jamie."

Chapter Sixty

I try not to dwell on Wilson's last words, all the way over to Mr. Jones' grain store. I could get hanged. Anyone could get hanged. Only trouble is that I am less of anyone than most people out in the world. I ain't ever seen no white man hanged.

"You look to be deep in thought, Jamie," says Jones before I reach his store.

I pull up to the high-curbed store in the village. During this time in the summer it is usually much dustier on these dirt streets. This year it is just muddy, wet, unending rain each day like clockwork after the sun's been blazing hot for hours. Only the wet does not even come close to cooling things down. Kind of the same as arising after a good night's sleep only to realize it doesn't much matter. The person whose property you are does not want you to miss a day of work. He has got to get his full use out of your body and –

"Wilson tells me you were wondering on what life is like in the western parts, Jamie." Jones has sacks of grain, oats and barley straddled over each shoulder.

"Oh did he ask you that?"

"I just like talking about the country out there. It is a dismal, rough life. But you ain't gonna see prettier mountains and the game has no end in those foothills. Just look out past that little mountain you live on. Others times I get to thinking, wondering who would the polite people of Charlottesville stare to see some of the females out to the west come to service in their shifts and short petticoats only, barefooted and bare legged – without caps or hankerchiefs – dressed only in their hair, quite in a state of nakedness is counted as nothing. There they all sleep altogether in common in one room, and shift and dress openly without ceremony. And the men, from the times I visited, I noticed that they appear in frocks or shirts – no shoes or stockings."

I let out a long slow breath. He's not talking for any other reason than to hear the sound of his voice. Jones looks out in the direction of the place he speaks of as if he is already there. I wait for him to turn around and look at me.

"Nine bags this time. This should be enough. You

got me to talking and I played slave for a bit. You, Jamie ain't done nothing but listen." He slowly looks me up and down before his gaze rests on my ankles.

Chapter Sixty-One

"What are you staring at Jones?"

He doesn't answer for a while. I keep moving, pick up a pile of new hemp rope that was on my list and lies coiled on the platform. Then I grab some wooden barrels fresh and tangy with the smell of new-cut oak slats awaiting the taste of hard cider soon to be stored inside.

"Those hens at your ankles look to be as full and quiet – and worn out – as much as any hens could be."

"What you done with that new file I swapped out with you the other day?"

I don't let his question rattle me. "I got some fine work to do on some of them nails Massa Jeff wanted what will be used for that new parlor of his, needing real smooth ends on them."

"Aw, horse shit, Jamie. You know that answer of yours needs to be loaded right on top of that." He motions with his thumb in the direction of a horse dung pile toward the back of his store.

Before he can say another word I pull a few nails from out of my pockets. Love these new britches that have pockets in them. "Have a look, Jones."

"So you say these with the smoother, flatter top you used my file on?"

"Just set them in the overseer's vise and worked

on them real lightly. You don't and the head just files right off of them."

"File's got more uses than just smoothing out leg irons, then."

I don't reply. I let it go like that morning half moon drifting behind the clouds, one that nobody else notices unless they have not a care in the world.

Chapter Sixty-Two

Back at my work shed I notice Gray going about his tasks. He caught a mouse yesterday, teased the thing pitifully just like Jones does with his words on my use for the file. The birds are silent this morning. Not even a red bird to brighten my morning by making his entrance. No. That crested bird that's gray-green, that catches mosquitoes and lives in a hole at the top of the walnut tree. He whoops his comical weeps up in those tall trees, white oaks.

I open my chest, one that I have the key to but no one even realizes that it is a chest with a key. Riffling the papers in the cool morning breeze I know this time will be, of course, different. I got a map of the territory to the west. Still recall the words of Tom from years back: "A map can make all of the difference, you see where you go and use it to love your life."

How does a slave love his life?

"Nice chest, Jamie. Why you closing it up so quick?"

As if to placate Wilson, I unlock it and show him my coins, all my greenbacks.

"OK. I see now." He sounds satisfied.

I don't tell him about my seven-inch knife just under those rags. Slaves cannot have arms, of course.

"Care to join me for some cornbread and coffee, Wilson?"

When he knits his brow to show I better get to work, I reach down and shake the bucket of nails for his pa. "Just a half tin cup I guess. Your coffee tastes like it's made from that dirt on the floor."

"Not given much to work with. Careful, it's hot, Wilson."

"Not really that hot anymore. Maybe when it was hot it tasted better than this."

I give him a hard look, hold that and then swallow mine with one big gulp. "I'm not going to have to put up with your ill will and ill humor much longer, Wilson." This slips out in a whisper which from the look on Wilson's face, he apparently has not heard.

He tries to sip some more and then with a sheepish look, follows suit with me and gulps down the rest. I wait for his eyes to wander down to my ankles and the steady work I've done lately with the file. But he seems distracted by the mosquitoes biting him far more than me.

The wild-looking tiger-striped cat meows inquiringly at the doorway further distracting Wilson. I look down at my hand to see a red-bellied mosquito fat with Wilson's blood, no doubt. Somehow it makes me feel a closer human to him even if by law his father has every right to extract the blood – in much larger amounts – from me and far more violently. A skeeter's needle mouth is no leather strap by any stretch.

"Thank you, Sir for the...what did you say that was? Coffee?"

"You are most welcome to it any time, Sir," I lie.

There ain't gonna be an anytime much longer. Just like when Tom showed me in the Notes book of Massa Jeff and how he feels slavery's gotta go but has to be done with no haste, in time, no matter how much haste we slaves have got to show before sunup right up until sundown. Massa feels too, that no matter how much time goes by we blacks aren't disposed to writing poetry – such talent just is not in us. I won't be the one to tell him that working sunup to sundown doesn't lend itself so much to sitting and thinking let alone writing poetry, especially since it is an offense to teach slaves to –

"Jamie? Those eyes of yours got that glazed-over look once again. Just wanted to say you sure have everything all tidy and neat laid-out, real nice in here. What's the occasion?"

"Just tired of staring at all the untidiness all the time," I lie once more.

Wilson doesn't linger in the doorway like tiger-stripe. Tiger-stripe sidesteps quickly. Wilson's footsteps thump down the path for a time.

The file scratches the inside of the iron rings on my ankles. I pause and hear Wilson's steps continue down the path. I wait to hear him stop and try to figure out what the filing is, but he does not and his steps trail off into nothing though the mosquitoes he attracted continue to dog my cheeks. I do not mind. If they want to take my blood in that itchy but painless way, they are welcome. The only sound reaching my ears now aside from the filings I do at my ankle, comes from the cicadas, though they are surely not nearly as loud as last year's.

A dove sounds mournful far off nearly out of earshot. "Are you warning me, Mr. Dove? Or are you simply echoing the words of Master Jefferson when he discovers his top nail maker has once more disappeared?" Cicadas gain in volume as if to tell me I am mad in my plan to try escape once more.

Gray sets a mangled featherless bird swarming with maggots and my feet. He stares into my yes waiting for my praise. Tom's explanation – from one of his pa's books on nature – seeps back into my mind. The writing in that book told him house cats do as such not to show off or give us a gift as much as that they feel we are so helpless, they must feed us.

"No, Gray, I can think of better things to eat. Even this here slave has not needed to stoop low enough to feast on rotted bird peppered with crawly worms."

Gray stares in my eyes waiting for my praise. "If it is, in fact, praise you seek, you gonna have to find someone else to do that, Gray. Do not be so sad, my friend. Your pa's gonna be happy when he's gone."

Chapter Sixty-Three

I forgot to leave it open. The door to my cabin stays open so much that I worry at times – such as now – when the door is closed, well, people may get to thinking something's going on inside.

I see through the cracks in the pre-dawn light that Gray's comfortable out in the grassy place near the edge of the path. The tiger striped cat for all his whining like he's never happy has been more of a companion than Gray lately. Stripe is quiet now, staring into my eyes like he be judge, jury, sheriff and overseer all in one.

"Mama always said people find a way to be happy. You be happy, Stripe. Sure don't sound like it. People are here to make themselves happy – get shoes near as nice as the pairs Pa used to send me over the years. A little thing, not much to make a person happy. Slave and happy. How, Stripe, do I use those two words in the same sentence and – ”

"How indeed, Jamie? Who the hell you talking to in there?" Wilson's up damned early.

Just glad I waited on the leg irons till just the right time of day. Thump. "Did I hit you with my door just then?"

"No. Why do you ask?"

"Not sure. For someone listening in on me I figured you needed to be near the door."

Wilson peers into the dimness of my cabin. Stripe is all over me of a sudden. His eyes lower as he glances at me, not bothering with the fly on my ankle.

"You talking in here to a cat about the meaning of happiness?"

"You take companionship wherever and whenever you can get it."

"Speaking of happy, you never let yourself be happy. I never seen you at any of the Sunday outings Massa Jeff plans – ever."

So much to say. People will find a way to be happy. Life finds a way to come forth like a watermelon vine growing out of a trash pile when no one expects it. I can't see happiness being anywhere near a place that I am owned more than a hammer is. At least with a hammer, file, cutters or tongs if they're mislaid – free – no dogs are set to tracking them. They can lie in the tall weeds unfound for ten years – a hundred years and no one raises a fuss.

"What's going on in that head of yours, Jamie? You

never answered my – "

"Oh, was that a question, Sir? Well, what I think you ask is what on earth could be stopping me from just finding some happiness, somehow like all them other folks."

"I suppose. You make it all complicated."

No, I think to myself, I make it simple if you would listen, Wilson. "This cat has a job, it be catching mice and birds – which are silent this morning for some reason. That mosquito sucking blood from your wrist has a job, bloodhounds have a job – tracking down men and I got a job, making nails. I don't much like my job. Pa could have a white man's job of going from cabin to cabin making shoes for all needing them in each of those families, but the color of his skin – his being property be all there is keeping him from doing as such, though he still can make shoes as good as any man, white or black. But that doesn't matter. I will not make searching for or forcing myself to find happiness in my job. That shouldn't be a job. It ought to just happen like a melon growing out back in the trash of this place where no one's expected it."

"I don't understand you, Jamie."

"Didn't ask you to, Wilson."

Chapter Sixty-Four

I set the bucket out by the front of my cabin as always and pick up a handful of nails, squeezing hard the mass of iron formed into a slender particle that in turn will soon be creating something else altogether. Up on the hill, through the cleared woods I see the house on the little mountain, Monticello.

A pair of candles flicker in the two side windows. They look to be burned all the way down to the very stub, just like my time here. That house is here because of my hands, never mind the nails themselves; I am the tool and I note this to myself.

A blue jay calls his annoying warning. "Up far too early Mr. Blue. You need to just get back to sleep like the rest of them." Cicadas sound like I imagine the ocean to sound like. Tom used to say his pa said it was so, the way the sound comes and goes, waves coming in, crashing on the shore and quietly going back out. I grab another handful of nails, one in each hand now, then throw them into the bucket – the largest bucketful I've ever done. I hope they appreciate it.

The ankle irons have places on thcm so worn, that now, as I run the file on them, there is barely a sound. I keep working at a crease formed by my thumb and index finger and the gap I've made. Then the break in the captive circle of iron about the bottom of my leg all these months is busted open, wider still when I push it. The skin there is tough and calloused, but tender, too, and painful if just the wrong amount of pressure brushes by.

Out in the trees I find my money stash. I place the coins into my money belt and put the rest in sacks tied on the inside of my pants. My papers I fold into my belt's remaining empty pocket too.

"You be up really early, Jamie."

"Well, what are you doing up this early, Jonah?"

I blink in disbelief at Jonah's groggy face. He has no clue what I am about, does not gaze down at my legs lacking their irons or the fact that for being probably four in the morning I don't look at all as if I have come out to empty my bladder and then get back to sleep in the precious hours before sunup. "Sorry for your pains of late, Jonah." I rub his shoulders hard. His eyes blink shut.

"Ouch! Watch that spot. Never healed right since that day I passed out from Lily's lash."

"Sorry, Jonah. Now you get back to bed. We are all going to need our strength in the morning."

"What? You don't sound like you, Jamie."

I give him a tight hug. And don't know what's come over me. "That be even less like me. Sorry."

Jonah nods. In the dark I can barely make out the features of his face but I can tell he knows now. "Godspeed, Jamie. Don't know what the hell that means. Heard the white folks say it to Massa Jeff when he left once for a long trip."

I cannot think of words for that and leave it at that as I leave Jonah alone at the base of the huge tulip tree I have always loved. Cicadas and their wave-making sounds have quit all of a sudden. Out in the field, lit by the clouded moonlight, Gray runs in my direction. "No, boy. I'm taking ya back to the cabin again." When I close the door he stays within. Not hard to fool a cat. Hounds howl in the distance to remind me of the animals I do need to fear.

Chapter Sixty-Five

A blue jay cries out a lackluster warning as if he's sleepier than poor Jonah when I left him hours back and a wren gives his chirpy caution as if to echo that of the jay. No argument whatsoever from the dove cooing out all mournful-like. "You don't have to sound that way Master Dove. Do I look sad?" Lately I got this spring in my step with the ankle irons gone. I feel like I could jump up into those puffy clouds looking close enough to touch. But I have no time to think on such things as this.

What shall I think on as my legs keep a steady pace like a busy hammer on an anvil making more – no – not nails, Jamie.

I think on stuff that Tom said years back, just before he was banished, smiling as he always did at the words certain unalienable rights, truths; but we both agreed that no truth has become more self-evident than that all men are created unequal. Why does a man who is so well-traveled, educated and widely read not understand this simple fact? I am, in fact, a man, not a piece of equipment and if my equipment-hood is taken away why can I not be a man in his eyes, one who can co-exist with him, a white man in this world which I was born to as well?

The air is sultry and close. I remember Tom telling me that word. That's the time when even a breeze fails to lift the spirits. This breeze right now is barely a whisper hardly worth thinking about but better than nothing.

I draw close to the Jones supply store I know so well. Out back the least valuable of the foods stay out in wooden baskets and bushels. Who's gonna bother stealing a sweet potato or an onion – and why? There are whole piles of them here, enough to feed lots of families and people. I stuff just a few, a sweet potato, white potato, onion, carrot, and a handful of radishes in my sack.

"Why would anyone do that?" The sound of Jones freezes me to my spot, until I realize he is talking to someone just inside the doorway.

"I haven't the slightest notion. And I know that is not any way to answer you." Both men start laughing and I see Jones still backing out of the doorway while engaging the person he's speaking with.

Why would he even need to gaze out this way? Is he expecting to see an onion, potato or corn ear thief? I grab an ear of corn just as that thought comes to me.

Chapter Sixty-Six

Not long after Jones nearly saw me swiping some of his vegetables, I'm out on the pasture he has for his horses. An open shed, well-used and starting to weed over, contains weathered saddles that look ill-used over many, many years. An idea flashes into my head, a burst of lightning uncontrolled and sudden out of the summer sky. I think of all the free men I encountered over the years. None were on foot, ever. They are too busy and important for that. I swear I hear the nails being pounded out in the distance. Could it be? No. It isn't the nails being hammered but that sound still echoes around in my brain. I shall feel joy when it no longer inhabits that space.

I have my answer to my wonderings. A broken, worn saddle straddles an old stump. As if to point to the possibilities of that saddle, an old horse grazes just beyond the stump, pricks her ears when she becomes aware of me but does not look up.

"It weren't nothing saddling you up, Independence," I whisper. "Don't know if that be your name, I doubt it. But that is what I'll call you from now on." Now I am heading down a path that looks as if it widens into a well-traveled road. This saddle feels worn and smooth beneath me and my back – long used to walking on my own two feet – adjusts to the feeling of sitting while moving, as this old horse walks along. I spur him on and note that he seems to crave such a new freedom as this, nearly as much as I do. Can something be spurred when the rider isn't wearing spurs?

"Where do you think you be going?"

The voice startles me near as much as it makes the horse jump. Something deep inside me pulls out words that Tom said once. He told me once his mother Miss Sally told him that people who drop their eyes when talking to you most likely aren't speaking the truth. "Business over in Lynchburg, Sir. Then on into the mountains."

The man, with his long, greasy hair pulled into a tail tied at the back of his head, lowers his musket still eying a squirrel he'd decided not to attempt a shot at. He does not hold his eyes on mine as long as I hold mine on his.

"Looks like you had a good chance with that one. One over there, too. But you got some competition. Hurry, don't be late."

"What?" His reply sounds annoyed.

I motion with my arm toward the squirrel gazing down on the whole scene and now making his squirrel's scratchy sounds. Then I let go of the reins a moment and point directly overhead to the red-tailed hawk not far above in the humid sky. Its ragged scree surprises us both. Perfect timing, Master Hawk.

"I have never seen one like you what know so much about the goings on here at the woods. Can't rightly see why you be heading to a mud hole like Lynchburg. What be your business there, in what some have taken to calling the seat of Satan's Kingdom?"

"Better let you take those squirrels if you be serious about it." I don't wait for him to debate or question but spur my horse on, not looking back. Shortly, gunshots confirm my boldness paid off. His horse remains tethered to the young tulip tree beside the man. More gunshots. "Just get me from out of your head, Sir." I smile. Cork screwy teakettle call of the wren seems to tell me life can be fun, unexpected and completely predictable in its unpredictability. I smile to myself that this tactic of mine seems certain to work.

I hear a church bell drift up my way from below. Even if I can't see the things of man and God, I can hear them and smell them. The smell of bacon frying somewhere below make it hard to keep on my horse.

Chapter Sixty-Seven

Several weeks of travel later, the ridge ahead invites me with up its cragginess. That same land looks as if it's better if two level feet can be held on it at one time. Strange thing is the smell of bacon, frying someplace is much stronger up here. I close my eyes and let the memories, all of them, sweep over me. We had fat back more than we ever had bacon. Bacon meant holiday times, if a few extra hours away from work can be called a holiday.

Bam! I see the smoke from the musket explosion and then see the barrel from where the sound came.

"You look to be a long way from home, Sir, and up here is a place where you ain't got no business anyhow." The man has sandy brown hair reaching down all the way over his eyes. He brushes it back as if to get a better look at me. "No satchel made of leather, I see – good."

I marvel at how well he blends in with the rocks, leaves, trees and bushes all about the place. Everything he wears seems like it comes right from this place, the rock-strewn land swallowing us both. "You've had something about your ankles for some time," he adds. "They don't look right, not the full meat of the rest of your legs."

"Some have some things they simply must take care of," I blurt. He notes the surprise in my eyes at his words. Not sure why I said what I did. Gray does a better job at concealing his thoughts and actions than I just did and he's rather simple-minded.

"Well, I don't really care what the hell you are doing up here, but if anything comes out with that," he motions with his chin to a huge mossy boulder with a thin stream of smoke wafting from a narrow opening to one side, "and I can't be saying I won't find a way to act on what the cause of those scrawny ankles of yours may just be."

For someone living far up on a lonely rocky mountain, this man knows something of the world without.

Boom. Smoke again. I turn and see a pair of squirrels tumble from the thin branches of a shagbark hickory tree. "Didn't quite make it to that chestnut they were heading to; that's where all the good nuts are, not in this one or that mocker-nut hickory beside you. They don't call them mocker-nuts for nothing."

"For someone alone you sure like to talk." I feel a bit too shy to be saying as much so soon after meeting. I hear a distant wave of cicadas crashing on the inner shore of my ears before receding into a buzzy hum. But in this place I hear very few of the creatures which fascinated old Gray at times.

"You be mouthier than any white man I have ever met. Damn it. I like that. Remember what I say now. Here is my name. Ferguson, Patrick Ferguson – same name as the one who was a redcoat. He was a brave man, but wasn't too lucky down at the battle on some place called King's Mountain where they killed him.

"One of his own ladies, a lass he had as one of his washerwomen, told the rebels he was wearing a red and white checkered shirt, which was his undoing. Our President once said that that hour-long fight was the turn of the tide. That may be the only thing his slave-holding self has right. Though the other Patrick fought for the other side, he couldn't be all bad. Before that, Ferguson fought up at a place called Brandywine where he had General Washington right in his gun sight – said he just couldn't pull the trigger to shoot a man in the back. Ain't that something? Don't mean to change the subject, but what would your name be?"

"I'm James. Some like to call me Jamie. Ain't no never mind which you prefer to call me," I call to him. But he surely is already out of earshot with the pair of squirrels in one hand and musket in the other. His shot settled down even the cicadas. Owl does his who-all call. But other than that and the chirping of some wayward sparrows, it is lonelier than the devil at this place. Lonely does not have to be so bad; better lonely than being someone's property, I reckon. Sounds like a word Patrick would use and I wonder how close reckon is to well, wonder.

Chapter Sixty-Eight

Later, Patrick lets me stay in his shed on some

straw and rags while his family, a wife and two little boys, stay inside their cabin. The air feels cool enough up here in the higher land for a smoky fire having to be lit within the place. I can tell the wet firewood isn't letting his fire burn quite as good and smokeless as it should.

I start to get back to my wondering as I lie here amid the soft stuff cast out into this shed, I think on Gray and even Stripe. They would never wander off. They are like those slaves that would never think to run off, cannot even see the point to it. When presented with the idea of it, they would just lick their paws and legs like Stripe was wont to do and settle down in an old chair to get more comfortable, even more unknowing of the world surrounding them. And thank you, Tom for that word 'wont' I think I used it right. You said it had something to do with a person or thing being used to doing something in that way. No, Master Jeff, you be right, I ain't no poet as Tom says you always pointed out to people in your letterings, but that isn't because I can't be one or don't want to be one or this black skin of mine makes it plum impossible–

"Jamie!"

The word sits me up straight more than the chill that's came over me in here God knows how many hours ago. "What is it, Sir? Patrick?"

"I heard them hours back. Been listening to them getting even closer bit by bit – even above Becky and the boys' snorings."

"Who is them?"

"Just listen."

I wish it was the sound of Stripe's carrying on, his meowing and face-to-face glances while Gray sits nearby. Desire that this were the sweet dream to come to life as I rub their necks to shut them up. But now I hear the bloods, too, sure as the breeze is starting to whip up the leaves just outside this tumbledown shed. "Got garlic and cloves in my shoes and all through – "

"You ain't gonna throw them off with that until they be much closer. They be coming on steady now. They must have spoken to the revenue people – those collectors of taxes for a product I make by the sweat of my brow in order to feed my wife and children – to know this place."

I feel Stripe's claws on my leg, the panicked feeling I get when he does that all of a sudden with no warning and I want it to stop.

"You don't need to worry."

"What?"

"I see it in your eyes, Man." Patrick motions with his hand.

Through the blackness I follow him until the soothing sounds of the rushing creek drown out the bloodhounds. We reach a spot where water spills in a sheet over a series of boulders. Suddenly I feel like that seemingly doomed cicada must have felt when he broke free of Gray's sure grasp and floated, fluttered half-eaten skyward. Gray looked up then in catty disgust at his failure, Mr. Cicada's triumph.

"Do you hear me?" Patrick asks. "I keep my best stuff in there behind that tiny waterfall, this narrow sheet of water. Never even told my Becky about it. When you reach what feels like the end there be an angling into a little place none could ever find. My best corn liquor still be in there. Room enough for you. Stay till I come for you."

I don't like closed-in places. This is about enough to make me give myself back to Massa Jeff. But I keep on with it. The last minutes before I made my way into this blackness stand etched in my mind, how Patrick scooped up sand, muck, gravel and rocks from the creek bed to cover up my footprints coming over to this place.

My heart's beating all lug-a-glug right now. Things simply do not feel right without and that's not just from the scared feeling I get. I am in here in the closeness that makes me think I'm about to get stuck at any moment, add to that worry the howls of the hounds filtering amid the whirring eternity of the crickets and grasshoppers. I almost long for those infernal cicadas to rise in a devil's chorus above the high-pitched buzzing. No. I feel lost and homeless. Feeling like a skeeter sucking a bellyful of blood red home from my body. But that ain't home. Home ain't something you suck up into your belly and fly away with.

"They's something about here. They start circling like that and they know something's amiss." The voice is faint, drown out by the waterfall and the gurgles of the creek.

"They go down in that water and you may as well take them hounds home." Another voice is anxious, on the verge of great anger, I can tell.

A hickory nut hits me on my shoulder for some strange reason. I look up. Above I see that this is more crevice than cave, a split rock with just a tiny swath of the dimmest light filtering down to me in this hole and making me feel lost. It feels like the day Gray walked toward me with a flapping tiger swallowtail butterfly in his teeth. Of all the things in the universe, Gray, why did you slaughter the one thing of such unquestioned beauty?

So here I am, trapped in the jaws of this boulder's cave teeth awaiting my capture. "Lord do you feel any love for me?" I whisper just under my breath. "Any love for me, whatsoever? Are you gonna crush me, let them crush me and my love for this free world like tiger swallowtail is crushed in Gray's jaws?" My voice catches all of a sudden right up at the top of my throat. I am praying aloud without realizing it, praying aloud when those with iron fetters for me are just feet away from my shivering body.

"Lord, is your universe the same cruel and random and heartless place to make me not any better than a poor, powdery helpless flapping insect – Tom told me that that whole family of things are insects – and –

"They ain't picking up anything here. They was thirsty. Just look at them."

"And it ain't like anything besides a possum or a coon or skunk could hide inside this boulder--"

"Oh, you'd know it if they be an old skunk in that rock. And you are correct. How would that thing be able to get back out once inside?"

That is the last I hear of them. I shut my eyes for seems my own idea of eternity. When I open them, there is spittle at the corner of my month telling me I dozed off, simply slumped over inside of a split rock. Would young Tom ever believe such adventures – or even Wilson? They'd doubt me and call me a liar, well maybe just Wilson would.

"You gonna live in that spider hole the rest of your days?" Patrick brings the smells of frying bacon and smoke some ways and calls in to me, unable to get much closer than he is now because the space is so tight.

"There ain't even enough room in here for the mosquitoes, let alone any spiders," I call back, rubbing my eyes to rid them of the crustiness at the corners.

"Plenty of mosquitoes out here. Maybe you ought to stay in there if you want to escape these whining devils."

I don't answer him. The squirming I do to get from this crack of a cave almost feels too much even to allow for any talking. A jay calls out his tired old warning and some sparrows sound ragged in their tweets while high above, out of sight, the goldfinch calls out his laughing notes of freedom to me, making me want to hug my own self.

"What are you doing, Jamie? Are you cold? Just asking that because in all this heat by the fire, you're doing a lot of squeezing of yourself with those powerful arms of yours."

"Naw. Just making sure this be really me that you helped save from them slave-catching bastards."

"Bastards doing their work and they are damned good at such work." Patrick's eyes have a relaxed knowing look, as if anyone could try to discover his secrets – his precious still in a crack cave in this solid boulder – but that they would also do better just to keep moving on.

Chapter Sixty-Nine

Morning needed to come far quicker for my throbbing stomach. The cooked oats, bacon and strong coffee I shovel into my mouth barely seem to fill my gut. Patrick knows me better than I know myself and grabs an empty wood bowl, scooping some more of the creamy mash of oats into it.

"I reckon those oats be mighty sweet for you,

Jamie." Morgan, Patrick's little boy seems to come to life with this revelation out of his little mouth.

"And how is that, Sir?"

"Pa, why is he calling me 'sir?' I'm just a little boy."

We all share smiles at his point. "Well, Morgan, are you going to tell me how these oats get their sweet?"

"If you promise not to tell the revenuers."

I nod in agreement and make a sign across my throat, which darkens Morgan's already determined face.

"See that old chestnut trunk yonder?" Morgan points to a massive tree trunk destroyed perhaps by a combination of old age, internal decay and the crowning blow of lightning from the heavens. "The trunk below the top is filled with tupelo honey."

"Not tupelo, Son, that one is low country tree. Remember when I told you the old tupelo is swampland tree? But trees are trees and that honey no doubt ain't nothing but wild flower honey, from a whole bunch of trees including the chestnut swallowing up that wild bee hive."

Morgan looks deflated all of a sudden.

"So you, Morgan be the one what discovered them bees and all of that sweet precious wild honey I'm enjoying?" I add this to brighten the conversation.

"Yes, Sir."

Patrick's eyes start to roll. He begins to talk and I put up a hand to stop him. A knowing smile spreads across his face.

Boom. Crack. Boom. The sounds of flintlock gunfire cease all talk.

"You like to go on an adventure with me, Jamie?"

Morgan's questions breaks the tension.

"No adventure, Son while that hunting's going on —"

"Or trackers on the prowl."

"Those trackers are probably ten miles away already, Jamie." Patrick eyes his forearm and slaps a pair of mosquitoes. "But just like these suckers they always seem to come back for more no matter what."

Chapter Seventy

The dry crackle of grasshoppers, crickets and the last of the distant cicadas lull me into a calmness only making the sigh of a bobcat eying me more shocking. My heart skips until I see only a wilder version of Stripe and Gray in those stoic yet menacing eyes. And yes, Tom I remember those words from you, most especially, stoic. The word does fit me like a doe skin glove these past years. As I walk along the bobcat moves low to the ground in the high grass I see and hunkers down while moving in compact motions with head held parallel to the ground.

"You ain't getting my hide. I ain't no quail, Master Bobcat."

"Who are you talking to now, Jamie?"

"I'm talking to the only living thing I see around, Patrick until you snuck up on me." I motion with my chin toward the brush where the cat has settled in.

"Oh yes, I see her now."

"Her?"

"Man cats tend to be much smaller and scrawnier

than that one. She's looking for a rabbit to bring to her kittens. And this morning I noticed you was gone before the sun. You weren't gonna tell us fare thee well?"

I feel my eyebrows arch reflexively at his words. Suddenly I crave the lilting laugh he adds to every other sentence, it seems. "I didn't want to wake your family, feel like you done–"

"Aw, coon shit. That's a load of it, for certain."

I hear Patrick's words and feel incapable of matching them with anything my mind can muster. The wren-bird scolds with a teakettle trio far too quick for my ears. Then a breeze near to chilly sounds as if it makes him rush through his sounds double-time. A goldfinch sounds faint on this breeze far above while all the rest of the bird sounds whirl together on this grand day.

"You didn't hear a word I just said, did you?"

"No, Patrick. Something about a place here, working with you?"

Patrick stares down at the ground scratching his head, the thick dark hair over his eyes for a time until he pushes it back up under his leather cap. "I could use your help with the traps for a time. For me to fool myself with thinking I can do this by own wits is as absurd as the President thinking he won his 1800 election fair Injun when all the slaves was counted as three-fifths of a person and all their votes in turn went to a slaveholder – him."

The words he just said fill me as much as peanuts shucked from their spidery shells. I know people don't usually eat them, they're mostly food for the hogs, but I find them filling and tasty if heated by the fire. Patrick's words taste real and meaty. But I dare not ask him how he may be privy – Tom says his pa always loved that word – to such information about Massa Jeff. In time and –

"What you be thinking, Jamie? Most likely your thoughts ain't what runs through my mind at times. Something on your face tells me you've had occasion to think on our second president from Virginia."

"No time for thinking on such as that, Patrick." I lie.

"Once again, something's telling me that that be a load of possum shit."

I can't help but smile at his words. My mind floods back to images of possums alive, dead or of a questionable state somewhere in between. Can't recall too much on the scat of a possum. Patrick catches my thoughts somehow and smiles.

"This thing called liberty which Mr. Jefferson has such grand ideas on always intrigued me," says Patrick, near as if he's simply talking to himself. "For someone so intent on it, it always struck me as curious that he had so many slaves, surely you knew that. And if those slaves supposedly were treated so well and love their time with such a benevolent master, why did some 30 escape to the British in the late Civil War, one in which Governor Jefferson fled his home, leaving us – his fellow Virginians to suffer and to find the Brits themselves crossing our fields?"

There is so much I want to say to Patrick, but I hold my tongue for now. I cannot let him know what I know about Massa Jeff as he should then add everything up. "Well, you still want me helping you with your traps for a time? I could do that until they come back checking on your stills."

"You didn't answer my question. Then again, I

guess it weren't truly a real question–"

"Maybe more a rhetorical one at that."

"Where you be learning such words as that?"

"Had a friend, Tom, what was good with words as such."

Patrick's face searches for meaning in what I've just said, tightening just a tad. Then it passes and I can tell he is back on practical matters at hand. "And if old Muskie and some of those others come by you, just tell them you be my slave."

Disbelief plays on my face as I stare at him with narrowing eyes. I feel my face open and relax just as a breath eases back into my lungs.

Patrick studies my reaction. "In this country, despite the distances, word gets around quick. There be less to talk on with me having a slave to help me out with my work than the idea of some black simply showing up and being here. Just the word, slave brings order to the world. Of course I gotta come up with some kind of story about an inheritance coming through just in case they question how in hell I'm able to afford you."

Order indeed, I think. "Even when I'm not a slave I must be one, be one to be free, even if that be a pretend slave. Appearances kept up for other people be damnable. It ain't none of my business what other people think."

"But it can be a bit of work controlling what they think and how they act. You can be a master of throwing the stone that is never seen, Jamie."

A great crowd, no – a murder of crows as Tom would take to reminding me – of noisy crows spirals around an oak grove as if to verify Patrick's words. Around and around they tug at the tethers to my heart, a heart that longs to be knotted to someplace where a soul cares about me and not only because my existence with them means gain, production, profit, money for them.

"You have no place to be, no plan or place to light out for if I be correct in my assumption – with the exception of avoiding recapture."

"Avoiding recapture would be my plan at this time." I feel small and insignificant with those words. What sort of plan is that? It is not a plan but a state of being. All of the grasshoppers and crickets in this meadow just below the craggy hill where Patrick and his family lives, sound muted and just barely heard, as if they wait for me to arrive at a plan for my life for the next day, week or even hour. "Avoiding capture is not a plan, Patrick."

"The Lord gave you strong arms and a solid chest and legs. Ain't never seen a man black or white tall as you. You better watch out for any Davids about. Matching all that with your quick mind has let you get out as far as you did. Look around. See many other escaped slaves?"

I take a quick look about and then shake my head. "What sort of animals do you trap?"

"That's a plan for you, well, the beginnings of one and –"

"Well, what have we got here?"

Patrick and I both turn about in surprise at a thin, dark-haired man with eyes darker than his hair if that can even be possible.

"I bought James because I needed help with my trapping," intones Patrick.

"Odd thing to purchase a slave for."

"He has other skills that will come in handy."

Patrick shrugs.

"What sort of skills?"

"Smithing. And my traps ain't gonna last forever. Always needing –"

"Told you before you need to dry and –"

"And I've heard all of this before. Come on, James."

Patrick and I don't talk for a long while as we walk along. Doesn't seem to be much to say. "Thank you, Patrick."

"Don't think it's over with Muskie. He don't even trust himself most of the time."

Chapter Seventy-One

Patrick shows me the signs of beaver in the area. Triangular-shaped tops of tree stumps of all sizes with clear gnaw marks means beavers have been at work. There is a clear difference between marks made with teeth and those made with an ax. The fact that the exposed wood is weathered and dark already means it may have been years since a beaver lived in this area.

Finally, we reach a spot where the slow languid waters of an upper pond, clearly constructed by a beaver, gives way to a series of rough troughs of open water. Patrick motions to the side of the creek. Gravel has formed tidy beach-like shorelines on one side. Just at the other side of a mossy boulder I see the rusty chain leading off from a loop-ended stake in the rock to the form in the water.

I lift up the chain and pull up my first beaver. The sight of the animal, a blob of thick lustrous fur, huge muddy pancake of a tail coming up out of the water catches my breath for a moment.

In the distance I hear the steady rhythm of a hammer beat, something needing nails – my nails, no doubt – pounded into it to make something, a house, a roof, a box or a wooden pallet to stack piles of fur from these watery animals.

After loading up this one and three more onto Patrick's back frame he calls to me.

"I have one more place to check." He points down into a ravine with a brushy-sided creek black with slow-moving water. "Didn't expect this one to have anything." He struggles with his load, but still motions to me to pull up the chain.

"Good God, is that a young beaver?" My question leaks out before I have a chance to think.

"Well, does the tail look anything like these?"

I shake my head. "Looks like the tail of a rat."

"Yes, Jamie, it be a rat of sorts – a muskrat."

I pull it up and notice another chain. That one yields an even larger one when I pull it from the water.

"These are actually more valuable than the beaver pelts though the beavers are getting much harder to find nowadays. I've even heard beavers have been trapped out of everywhere else in Virginia."

The initial shock of the brutality of the traps and their unfortunate prey eases a bit. The rusty iron of the trap's not too far off from that of my making of the nails all these years. Mr. Beaver died a quick death at the hands of the iron. I died a daily death at the iron I worked with to survive. Survive? Was it survival or marking time for an existence no one can truly grasp, pain numbed by the meaningless of the nail count to me, the joy, smiles, profit and food it meant to everyone else and –

"Looks like we got some company a coming on."

"I don't recall you having a man with you when we visited you last." I smell the rum on his breath from many paces back. The tracker looks exhausted and surprised all in one.

"Where are your bloodhounds, Sir?" Patrick skirts around the initial statement like a fox sparrow averting capture by the kestrel, thrashing deeper into the life-giving blackberry brambles. Miss mourning dove intones her dreary, toneless opinion of the day.

"If you have yourself a slave you need to show the papers proving the legality of the sale."

"What if I don't have the papers? I did have a fire awhile back. Burned all my personal effects."

The tracker's eyes go from sour to tired. The bloodhounds moan in the distance. Patrick fingers his rifle and looks at me as I hold mine. "Suppose we shall see about it all. Ain't gonna be many beavers left for too much longer. All of Europe demands the felt for them fancy hats gentlemen need to all be in one style."

This statement explodes in my mind like the wren's bright tea kettle cry bursting from the brush pile. If I can hide out, I can find where the last of the beavers are hiding and make my own way.

"I shall be back," says the tracker.

"And we shall wait here for you, Sir." Only the muted sounds of the field's grasshoppers buzz on for us.

Chapter Seventy-Two

I know that old Gray is no doubt wandering around right now sniffing at the leaves on the ground and still turning his fussy cat nose up at some egg yolk left out for him on a plate. I find myself thinking of him more often at times like this when I have lots of time on my hands. I rest my body in the highest branches of a massive chestnut tree. The wind takes the thick branches and both gently rocks them, though at time sees the need to whip them as best as she can too. I think on how something as unseen as the wind, or the water in the creek just below me in the hollow can still have such power to move seemingly solid things.

A crow cry far above shakes me from my thoughts. Mr. Crow wants me knowing I sit in his favorite tree I suppose. The closed in feeling of Monticello, the little town trapping me, sapping me at that place diminish for certain far up here. The word diminish came to me just at the right time, Tom. Thank you, my friend.

Chapter Seventy-Three

My eyes open upon a white-blue sky, more white in most places than blue. I am two and a half days journey from Patrick's place and my bag has just three beaver pelts lying within its space and nothing to brag on either. I retrieved the gland with the castoreum as Patrick showed me, and reset the half dozen traps at strategic places not far from where I took the beavers. I used the scented castoreum – with a powerful smell of vanilla – just as he showed me. But Patrick is correct. There ain't gonna be many more beavers in this country for too much longer.

A great commotion sets up over toward the brushy woods. Some bobcats go about having some kind of fight. The hisses and screams jar me from my peace. A fly lights on my hand, wing all askew like no fly I've ever seen before. "How do you manage to get on, Massa Fly? And you can thank Tom for that fancy word, askew. Gonna say askance but that means something else I cannot rightly recall. In any case, that wing of yours don't look right. Can you possibly help me to get some eggs and pan bread this morning?"

I feel faint somehow and feel a panic sweep over me with this sudden lack of control. On the ground I suck in a breath to calm me and then remember how little sleep I had last night. Then nothing, for a moment.

"Who the hell you talking to, Man, and who was gonna get you that food?"

The voice feels part of some dream I fell into, too unreal to make me aware it is real. Sounds of a wayward cricket contrast with the steady screams of distant jays. But he, a black man kneeling at my side, pulling off his hat and scratching his head, sits me up straight all of a sudden. "When did I speak?"

"You spoke for a time and then you faded. I sat over there watching to see what you were about. Thought you liked to about died."

Something about the man is real familiar. I cannot bring myself out of the dream I just had, with Tom there laughing at me and this well-built man gently shaking my shoulder to see if I'm still among the living.

"Do I vex you, Sir?"

"Tom? Tom Hemings –"

"No. That's not my name."

When he sees my face drop, eyes cast down for a brief moment, a cork-screwy wren call, distinctive to this place, seems to bring a cleverness to his eyes.

"Tom Woodson, Jamie. And I do vex you, don't I?"

The next moments blur with feelings while only the wren provides any reality. Then we grab each other's shoulders and embrace, years melting away. I grasp for his hands, the ones that yanked Gray's tail and shoved me into the dirt and brought me food, too. We do not talk. We just sit, the scenes from years past matched in each other's smiles and eyes.

"I got some folks for you to meet. River's my property, mine and Jemima's. But maybe just in words."

"Words," I whisper. "Your papa always had all them amazing words, Tom."

"In the end that's all they were – words – not real life."

Chapter Seventy-Four

The cabin stands at the end of a long narrow meadow with steep hills, not really too far even from any of the structure's walls. Down below in a small, rugged ravine, a stream rips a space in the dark earth while tumbling on its way amid rocks and boulders. These gray chunks continue wearing out of the black earth showing from under the tall grass.

"What did you bring him here for?" I hear the woman's voice soon after Tom goes into the cabin. The words of Tom's deep voice when he speaks are too quiet for me to catch. At the far end of the cornfield two children, a boy and a smaller girl, work a mound of dirt with some sort of hand tools. Looks to me to be a child's version of a fort from some other land. I think of Tom's mind and the stories he must have shared with the children. It all fits and –

"You daydreaming once again Jamie? Of course you always had your work done long before the rest."

"No. Never daydreamed, Tom."

"Well, what are you doing then?"

I motion with my chin to his children. "Just be adding things up, is all. They look to be building some sort of castle or fort. What child in Virginia knows of such?"

"I do tell them of Papa's travels, things in his books."

"Why do you call him 'Papa' still, after all?"

"No, sir. Enough, Jamie, that is all far too long ago," intones Tom.

She pushes open the door with her back as she has a board with cooked oats, bread and bacon on top. On the broad stump beside me she sets it all down. "This here is Jemima. Jemima, this is Jamie."

"Sir." Jemima nods as she whispers the word. "River, put down your sewing and bring out that pot with the coffee and some cups."

I hear rustling inside, things set down I suppose. Then the clatter of cups just mentioned arises.

"Do you like your porridge, Jamie? Sorry we cannot offer you a bit more than this. We need to get more pigs soon, that be the last of our bacon too."

"Mmmm." I feel my stomach with my hand as I fill my gut as well. This proves enough of a reply.

"Guess you were hungry," Tom chuckles.

When I turn around she sweeps through the doorway. Her eyes are down, intent on keeping the contents atop the wooden tray on the plate. I move the first tray to the ground. She nods her approval as her eyes shift in Tom's direction. I wait for Tom's introduction but at once feel transported to another far off earlier time. I'm Tom. Your name is Boy.... The innocent finality of those words from way back when crash upon this present scene like a huge rotten oak limb falling to the earth whether a person stands beneath the tree or not. "I take it this must be River."

"That be my name, Sir."

"One could say as well, 'That is my name,'" I smile broadly, if not stupidly in an attempt to overcome the preaching tone of my words, the very first words from my mouth to this person I have never even met before. Then I hold my racing mind. Person? This is Tom's slave and truly under the law no person. I stand not even under the law but as stolen property, contraband if you will, even if I am doing all the stealing myself.

Teakettle. Teakettle. Teakettle. This wren sounds more distinctive, assured and alive than any wren I have heard in a long while. Some of that may just reflect my present condition.

"Jamie? Do you have anything else to say to River?"

"River, I feel the first words from my mouth to you should not be those of my correcting you. You be, no, are – a bee is a busy insect with the honey or the stinger – even finer to look at here before me than the picture with words Tom painted for me."

"What?"

I quickly shake my head at Tom before River looks

up at me once more. When her eyes meet mine I notice that despite her light complexion, her eyes are nearly black, making them even more striking when they hold onto mine. She hefts the wood buckets by their rope handles and nods in submission as if to excuse herself to go down the steep bank toward the pool of the creek.

"You know far more grammar than the last time I seen you, Jamie. Laws are still the same regarding the teaching of a slave to read. If anything the laws are even stricter in the wake of Gabriel's Conspiracy."

"I be afeared to even ask about such a thing as that."

"There is nothing to be afraid of, Jamie. A freeman named Gabriel organized thousands of slaves to rise up and march on Richmond, to burn its capital building. Never forget ole Massa Jeff saying, 'We are truly to be pitied' and by we he meant, of course Virginia's white citizens for possibly losing their precious property and having to hold down a large population of potentially dangerous blacks. No harm ever come to the whites. Then some slave spilled the beans before anything came of the uprising.

"Thirty or more slaves and free blacks be hanged and Jeff, feeling right bad about things and the injustice of the court trials with hangings involving quite a few innocents, sent a bunch of those slaves involved to some place called the Sierra Leone Company Colony in Africa. He pointed out these were simply blacks from here wanting their liberty just as all men did during the late Civil War with Britain, only Sierra Leone wouldn't take them. So ole Gabriel's partners in attempted freedom were sold as slaves in the Spanish and Portuguese colonies. Three cheers for Jeff's plan to give blacks freedom – freedom for those slaves, bu only as long as it is not in the country of their birth."

I take it all in for a few moments. Massa Jeff's face flashes before me, always in thought, eyes as sharp as a squirrel's while carving up a nut recently excavated from the ground. And when the words do come from old Jeff, you can tell much thought has come just behind them. Yet could he still have things that wrong, despite all that thought?

"I only tell you all that information as a caution on how you may sound when speaking. Grammar, all proper-like rubs off as a part of that teaching process. Wasn't too long ago they'd say 'I want to learn you this or that' some in fact, still say that. Pap – no Jeff – said the new and proper way now is to say teach, not learn."

An unbridled Redwing gives his warning con-kor-ee sound down from the direction of where River is headed. His bird voice echoes the agitation I feel with Tom's words just now. I nod in a blank sort of agreement and raise a hand to excuse myself as I head down toward his property, with a most poetic name – River.

"She can get it. That's what –"

"No. I am a gentleman." I keep on my way down the steep hill I've already started at. River, for all her care, slips on the muddy path and goes sharply to a knee. One bucket hits her arm and topples, soaking her skirt more than halfway to her waist.

"Sir, you do not have to."

"No. Here." I pull her to her feet, brush off the wet leaves and am filling the bucket in one of the few pools of this rushing brook before she can speak again. I look up at Tom who has his fists on his hips. His face is a mask of uncertainty. "We are fine." I call up to him. "No need to help us up." The buckets are full to the brim as we gingerly make our way up the slope amid mossy slippery rocks and the treacherous mud.

"You are not my slave, Jamie."

"We could always send the money for your benefits from having me about, to your pa." The words feel strange flying from my mouth like a lucky bluebottle fly as a wren screams his displeasure at that fly what – no that – just escaped from its beak.

Chapter Seventy-Five

It took me three days to journey to this place and if there are beaver left in Virginia – anywhere – this, here is the place where they may just be. From this high plateau I spy the fires from houses and towns far below, just wisps of thin smoke trailing up for a time until the breeze carries the smoke off in another direction and all becomes invisible.

I can see any approaches below me, anyone making their way up here although there are places where the trees thicken up and allow a person to be hidden. Patrick has praised anything I have brought him and rewarded me with payments I have add to what is already in my money belt.

I think about the project back at the bigger river down the way from Patrick's place. A great chestnut fell and its solid wood I have dried out further and slowly but surely crafted my own sort of escape boat for rushing downriver.

"What you be thinking now, Jamie? My sneaking up may just vex you once more." Tom calls from the opposite side I've been looking. He sees my astonishment. "You didn't know that there be a way down that seemingly impossible ravine called the 'gangplank' that lets a body through to your aerie up here among the clouds."

"Tom. Yes, I suppose you will vex me the rest of my days." I am glad he pointed this out to me any any case.

"Quiet up here," he calls up to me.

"How is River?"

"You look to be taking quite an interest in my property lately."

I cannot bring any words out of my mouth to respond to that. It is kind of like the grab of my ankle or foot with a sudden bite by Gray, unprovoked and shocking in its own way. "You have a fine piece of property, as you put it, Tom."

"Let us simply keep it so, Jamie."

"Patrick told me Massa Jeff, your pa, once wrote 'All men are created equal,' some such thing fashioned as a 'Declaration of Independence.' I can tell I have not spoken unwisely with this."

"Words written by the young usually end up just that. One word that made much more of an impression on my young mind was one he wrote in the margin of his record book once. 'Pa, why did you write out FOUR right there,' I asked him. And with no hesitation from the one that wrote those other lofty words Patrick told you of, Jeff intoned: 'Oh that would be the guaranteed percent increase each year – annually is another way to put it – if my slaves keep on reproducing'."

"Reproducing," I hiss. "Like a chicken or hog what knows no better, a bluebottle fly leaving her maggots on the carrion." Or like you would have your property, River do, no matter what my feelings for her. "Would you have me be your slave, your property too, Tom, so that I can be with her?"

The air matches our feelings some way, a breathless, soundless and constricting gloom settles all about us. I wonder how Tom feels. For myself, I cannot breathe.

"I have no words for that, Jamie. This proposal of yours makes no sense."

"As much sense as your pa's Roman family, slaves all part of one happy family and well, I don't know what else to say."

"What the hell you talking about, Jamie?"

"Something I'm remembering your saying back when you were no older than your little boy."

"But you must remember, I use to parrot Pa's words and thoughts all the time."

Chapter Seventy-Six

Days later when back, far below at Tom's place, I think of the word parrot. I have learned over the years that this is the same as something said without any thought to the meaning of those words just spoken. I give young Tom more credit than the older version. He always seemed to comment thoughtfully on things Massa Jeff had said, things he saw around him that did not quite fit with those words, lofty words as he just called them the other day.

Bang. Bang. Bang. Teakettles take over from the wren between the hammering sounds. Tom hits the iron wedge with the iron-headed hammer to try to split his gigantic chestnut stump.

"Here's one tree that will always be here for us," sighs Tom. "The giant chestnut – indestructible, yet yielding when you need it to be, like a perfect slave, you might say. And like a slave, owned from cradle until grave, the wood from this perfect tree is used to build cradles, for when a man or woman is born all the way until it is used as their coffin when that same person finally goes to their reward."

He knows he's gotten under my skin somehow. In a flash I curse the chestnut under my breath and in a devilish whisper, will the great forests of them gone from Virginia and the earth. Tom's words echo that wedge he uses to split apart his chestnut stump, or split us apart from any closeness we once had years back. "Patrick no doubt will wonder on where I have gone and what has become of his traps."

Tom stares at me a moment, then nods and tugs on his cap as if to leave it all at that. He points to a huge wooden platter of food that the flies and hornets have discovered as well, knowing that I have a long way to travel back up the mountain.

"Here's some fresh hot coffee." River surprises me as I lean against the porch post looking out at Tom, now stripped to his waist as he rains his blows on the great chestnut tree stump. "Thank you, kindly, Ma'am!"

"Ma'am? I ain't no Ma'am!" River holds my eyes in hers unsure what she is seeing exactly in mine. I reach forward and slip my hand around her waist. She holds steady. But when I pull her toward me she lets our bodies touch. For that brief moment there seems nothing else in the universe except the two of us. We let out a sigh as one, near as I can tell.

Yellow-gold finch bird sings his jubilant song. Up and down goes the faint warble high above us until it breaks off, fragile as a kite-string brief as this moment must, of course, be.

"Well, will you be back?"

"What do you think my River?"

"I think you will."

You thought correctly, I muse, losing myself in thoughts of the moment until a pair of squirrels squeals and screams, tumbling, fighting all the way down the side of a hickory tree back behind the cabin. I spy a katydid right on the – "Just hold still, Sweetheart, do not – "

"Do not what? What is it?"

"Someone, something wanting to catch a buggy ride on your head."

River sucks in a breath and staggers back in fear. I smile and start to laugh. But before I can lift the stunning emerald creature to show her, the handsome insect bursts from my grasp leaving only the tall jointed leg behind. "Something wanted to be away from you more than you would be away from it." I point to the place where it has landed, on the trunk of the nearby hickory.

"The nasty thing."

"Seen far worse than that. Wish I had his camouflage. Your Massa, Tom, taught me that word."

"Guess he don't mind breaking the law to teach you things."

I leave it at that. No sense comes from arguing on anything. I want to say Tom taught me much when he was but a boy, the person I loved and remember, not the complicated grown man who I know would not favor me carrying on like this with his property. He has, as well much of the mystery, fogginess, if not down right insincerity – falseness – of his so-called dignified pa. All those words buzz around in my brain thanks to Master Tom, the younger.

"What goes on in that handsome head of yours now, James?"

I feel myself blush at the word, one I've never recalled used for either me or my head. The feeling passes as quickly as it came on. "Tom said that in his pa's book, Massa Jeff made clear that in the scheme of things the black African always remained an alien, an interloper in a land where he could sink no roots. King George III is the cause of this fault, Jeff says. To rid this land of all of us blacks is to be obedient to 'overruling Providence' which decreed us slaves should be freed, emancipated. But the plan for settling this Garden of the World never included us blacks in its midst. So it is of no avail for blacks to plead that the rights of man entitled them to remain in this land and partake of the liberty and material bounty that that country afforded."

River draws in a breath and looks into my eyes once more. "Well, I asked and your thoughts came tumbling out like rock rolling down a hill. You have more to tell. Your eyes show me that much for certain."

We cannot win with you, Massa Jeff, I want to tell her. Would she even understand? "You deny the right to enslave us, Massa Jeff I would tell him were he here and listening to me, but say we in turn have no right to reside in this country of our birth, a birth not into life but into being the same as a hammer, anvil, cart, bellow, butter churn or any other everyday possession."

Her face darkens, eyes narrowing. "These are words I know, but put together in this way I feel a blinding cloth has been untied from around my head and eyes."

"Far back we were from some place called Africa. But less far back, Massa Jeff – Tom's father and his kin were from places called Ireland, England, Scotland,

Holland or Germany. Yes, Massa Jeff's son Tom told me those names. Jeff would never know I learned all that, not in one thousand years. And I know numbers and ciphering too. Tom says ole Massa Jeff, he feels that he acts in concert with cosmic forces. But I say, after much time thinking about this, that those cosmic forces fly from out of your brain, not the will of any God's heaven, Massa Jeff.

"And I just don't know that black men possess the same sexual ardor for white women that orangutans possess for black women, which Tom also read in that book his father, Mass Jeff wrote. I don't know what an orangutan is but I see no difference in the ardor of one man for a woman be that man white or black; depends on the person."

"I think this orangutan you speak of must be some sort of hairy animal, orange like the fruit that he be named for."

I have gone too far. Too many words have may have spoiled the moment, like a fly buzzing around your porridge or soup at the supper table, keeping you from eating as you would like.

"I must a done something, you be all shy of a sudden," whispers River.

I do not let her speak anymore. We sit and watch the sun fade off beyond the western ridges. The new moon thin as a silver fingernail looks tethered at a striking lovely angle to the Evening Star. That is the one which Tom told me years back isn't a star at all but a planet, Venus, a wanderer like this earth itself, in the night sky. And like me. I whisper these things to River. Teach them to her in defiance of any Virginia law, a state taking part as a colony once in the fight for liberty from England, though now it has an odd meaning, indeed, for such liberty when it comes to persons such as me and River.

Chapter Seventy-Seven

I've got spring in my step this morning, on my way back to Patrick to deliver a nice haul of furs, as pelts I hear some speak of them. The marsh below Tom's cabin teems with muskrats and I actually trapped an astounding five beavers in the time there. I hear if you don't retrieve a beaver soon enough, just as with the katydid that gave up one of her six legs to escape my fingers, a beaver will chew apart its own leg or paw to escape.

At once I feel kin to both beavers and insects. I did what I had to in order to go free myself. Now I will save up my money to buy River's freedom. The plan makes my heart sing brighter and broader than any sparrow singing from the blackberry brambles this morning. I get a whiff of bacon frying far below, along the river, and I wonder how long till I have me a home such as that.

The sharp barks of a coyote are soon joined by others adding up to an ungodly howl all of a sudden. What they're doing up this early, with no moon out I haven't a clue. I think about what Tom told me of his pa. He told it in his words using a wolf as the creature, though – not a coyote.

As a boy Tom heard his father tell a Monticello visitor that the problem of having us slaves as the future comes on is like that of someone trying to hold a wolf by the ears. Whether that wolf is rabid or not, he did not say. But he did tell young Tom not to be worrying his head about anything with that. Tom says the importation of slaves from across the seas was made illegal by President Jefferson a few years back.

Only now that just means more of the reproducing slaves that are already here will be of even more value for growing cotton down in the Carolinas and Georgia as well as farther to the west. With this great chunk of land called Louisiana, bought from old Napoleon, means the French way of not letting families be broken up in sales or allowing blacks a patch of garden or testifying in court would be abolished under the new United States laws. I see that wolf Massa Jeff worried on, baring his yellow-white teeth, indeed.

Chapter Seventy-Eight

Later in the week I can hear Patrick's children laughing up at the top of the hill. In one small way I feel glad to be at this place, the closest to being a home that I have ever seen and which I shall no doubt ever see again.

The last of the season's skeeters bite my forearms with the vengeance of Lilly taking his strap to the boys. And where one comes on, by some kind of insect magic he brings on all his brothers to share in the feast. No. I recall young Tom telling me, when he did tell me things that it is the lady skeeter that drains the red from one's arm. The men aren't equipped as such. The things that stick in a man's is something the girl mosquitoes have.

"Hello, Stranger." Patrick approaches from out of the glade just before his cabin. "Looks like you might have something for me."

"Just wait until you see, Massa Patrick."

"I ain't your, nor no one other's massa, Boy."

"Who you calling 'boy?'"

With that we hug. Both feel maybe it has been just way too long since I've been back here.

Later Patrick emerges from his cabin with a huge bowl fashioned from light durable chestnut wood by his wife and now filled with steaming oat porridge. Tart crab apples sliced with cinnamon and honey on top add to the treat.

"Why can't the men that work for Massa Jeff be fed this way?"

"I don't know for certain," says Patrick.

I don't have the heart or mind to tell him that I wasn't truly wanting an answer to my question. Young Tom called it a rhetorical question. I let it go. Patrick no more knows about such as this than –

"Did you just mean that rhetorically?"

I smile at his words and shake my head slowly. "You just reminded me once more never to assume nothing."

"Anything."

"I like the sound of nothing, better, word without oblig --"

"Obligations?"

The bowl is so big it sits at my side here on the log for a time. I got back just before sundown and now with the glow of a campfire out behind the cabin, the peepers and distant owls sound extra soothing and right. "I can tell you be about to say something Massa – no – Patrick."

"Yes, well...oh never mind it."

"No. You said yes, Patrick, well, so go on with it,

Sir. You afraid I can't – "

"No, just don't know that it be something..."

"What?" Now I've gotta know. I mean, how could anything Patrick might say or do to me vex me? Jays taunt with their call, warning of something in this twilight time of day.

"You told me you worked making nails, right?" The bird's calls spur Patrick to let loose with something.

"Most definitely."

"You sound like a lawyer now. You know what wooden pegs are and how fast, easy and simple they are to make as well as use, don't you?" The sounds of an iron church bell far below in the valley drifts up to our ears as if to remind us both of the importance of iron for not only nails.

"What of it?" I ask.

"There is no good reason for Jefferson to work you slaves near to death making nails."

"Nails hold everything together in that mansion," I   suggest.
    "Mule shit. There is just one reason alone for them nails being used."

We both go silent for what feels an eternity. I suck in a deep breath. "Then say it."

"Tom ever taught you the meaning of this word, 'prestige?'"

"So being a show off is what you are saying?" I let his words, his thought sink in. Patrick knows not to ask me anymore nor comment as I let my mind drift painfully like a sharp pulled muscle in the back or side to Lilly's ungodly strap near to crushing the life from out of young Jamie Hemings and all of those damned nails to make a man and what he has, look and be the best.

"I guess I am just the opposite, if I might say rhetorically. I, Patrick, feel it's none of my business what people think. Had I a house they could think ill of me if it be held together with wooden pegs instead of nails. As, I suppose the sun's still coming up, come the dawn in the morning."

Chapter Seventy-Nine

I hear the voices of the family I have come to love far up the hill. Out here, voices travel and even as far off as they are their clarity matches that of the stars up here in the mountains far above any towns.

The children sound tired. Patrick laughs as he tells them something. They laugh even louder and the comfort in all of that, the surety in the midst of the terror and uncertainty of all the world without lets me drift softly off to sleep.

But this sleep comes not before a rusty-tailed hawk – up in the tulip trees above my lean-to here – screams softly, peppering the nightmares of any dozing squirrels or Gray were he here with me. Gray frantically shoves and nudges at his water bowl in an insane rush to get at something underneath, the living force he thinks inhabits a space beneath the saucer he quickly, surely spills all the water from in the process. For an instant, a darkness, like the rumor of bad weather seizes my body and mind. However, why, then, would he be shouting in the voice of a man, something sounding like 'Over here! 'Come look at this!'?"

My eyes snap open, voices from without my leafy lean-to crash in on my imaginary cat dream. I creep up the steep hill to see the thing I have always dreaded. A man on horseback and those on foot have up rooted Patrick's hard cider liquor still, his equipment and dumped it into the center of the meadow before his cabin which now has the doors torn off. A torch is lifted from a nearby fire and straw set near to the walls bursts into flames along with the edge of Patrick's cozy cabin.

Thankfully, no sign exists of Patrick or his family as I linger no more than I have to at the edge of this place which has become my home of late. My mind rushes ahead despite the tears blurring my vision. The hounds sound closer, all around as if they were brought here, brought to capture me at the same time Patrick and his still were seized.

The trail is overgrown but I know it well. It weaves down the edge of the ravine and twists back and forth in a mad rush to get to the water roaring below, white-black now from weeks or rain in the mountains miles away from this ground. I reach the steep slippery shore and pull back the brush pile on the bank. Only one of the three hand-carved boats remains. Patrick's way just before me reveals itself.

Abigail had her a small corn husk doll and that now lies at the edge of the water. I feel her panic when she realizes her precious little friend is not among her things in the escape boat. The handmade figure is soggy now with evidently no time left to retrieve it by anyone from the family. The baying hounds keeps me from weeping at the sadness of the little thing, the dream of a child who will mourn its loss perhaps on until she gathers her own grandchildren around the fire to tell of the precious plaything's life.

When I toss my bag in the canoe and jump in, my boat nearly capsizes. Only after a long tortured moment does the vessel find the way out into the rush of the water, the sound of which at the very least drowns out the cries of the hounds just up the bank. My fear of being captured once again, after all these months – no years – now lets me overcome my hesitation.

Chapter Eighty

The boat is much shakier in the water than I ever imagined it could be while I carved it. Then, the wood felt solid and nearly unyielding in my hands without the tools of Patrick to help me. I bob like a cork-screwy cap through the blur of dappled sunlight, whitewater and the blackness of darker pools off to the sides. As the river narrows the water deepens but goes no slower, not by much than in the wider places of the stream.

A squirrel does its twisted corkscrew squeal of anger in the trees above my head. The sound feels out of place amid the rush of the water over mossy boulders and crags along the shoreline. Just barely can I hear the hounds now, their howls trailing off amid the much louder notes of the chickadees and woodpeckers. Motion and balance, smells from the moist hemlocks, pines and tulip trees all about me let me forget about my worries about Patrick and his family and where I may end up come day's end.

Then a sound off from any of the others I have heard starts to fill my head. Above the growing roar of the water I hear the peter birds with their alerts head crests just overhead, seemingly oblivious to the dangers I endure below their bright black currant eyes. A bobcat screams on the hill to my left. To take my mind from the fears of the river I scan amid the leaves and see no sign of the creature.

Before too long I spy him – no her – sitting lion-like on a flat place on the bank up above. She stares down at me as if I have completely lost my mind. I wonder on that possibility too.

The roar of the water drowns out all other sounds and my dugout canoe feels as if it is completely confused by this new way of motion. I stab furiously at the water to keep the boat lined up – parallel, as Tom told me – to the creek's main flow but my efforts feel worse than futile as if extra thick leg fetters clap onto my ankles, ones no file could ever weaken.

A great dead limb bursts into my vision at the same time that a jagged boulder beneath the water strikes the boat's bottom hard. My ducking to avoid pummeling by the limb and the upset from below flips the tiny vessel. I resurface from the icy black-white water clinging for anything. But the boat and all my stuff have already rushed ahead and out of my feeble grasp.

In pure panic I gulp at the water, starting to fill my lungs. Fighting the awful sensation, I beat the wet with my arms and kick to stay up. When I spit and putter all the water I can from out of my lungs, the thought slaps me like an overly-friendly back pat. I am alive. I have not drowned or been pulled beneath the waves. In the midst of the terror of death, I live and control and keep floundering below the mocking jays screeching from just above, hawks and oblivious chickadees twittering their laughing chirp down through the leaves.

Mossy wet smells and mildew bring back memories and create new ones now. Just like Gray who always managed to free himself from the little belled collars I tied about his neck, I am free of the death embrace of these waves while riding in their midst. But

Gray's freedom from his bell collar meant death to a lady cardinal I grabbed from his teeth and paws and held while it convulsed its last death rattle. Now I feel I witness my own life in the midst of certain death amid these white waves.

Chapter Eighty-One

Somehow I retrieve some jerked meat from the pockets of my trousers and other clothes washed ashore. The night is freezing cold. I focus my mind on the one thing I can think safely about to warm me right now, River.

Still, I keep the feeling of yesterday going on. I am alive, just like the life buzzing all about me despite their conditions and despite how sorry I feel for myself, with mine. Sunshine hits a patch of ground where leaves are warmed now. Even out here, there is hardly else around except for a hornet that buzzing about the grizzly part of the greasy, wet beef jerky I left on the ground. The stuff does not stay long. Even a tiny six-legged creatures cannot tell a bad deal, rotted meat when it comes upon it.

I am thoroughly dried off now and well-rested, though still wrestling a fierce hunger. I head in the direction of the notched mountains I remember seeing much closer when I was at Tom's place. Tom will let me work for him until all is straightened out. Do not know if I shall ever see Patrick again. The thought takes a chunk from out of my chest. I came to think more of Patrick than I ever did of –

"Crack. Crack."

The sound of musket fire stops my thought. And

the sound's origin is nearly impossible to determine. Somehow this last thought puts spring in my step as never before. Wet leaves and pine needles fresh-fallen from the trees ease my world of worries, even those with the rifle fire, for whatever reason, going on down below. Then I see the reason.

A deer charges off to one side of the glade I have entered. It seems to charge half blind with terror and fear. Then it stumbles. Deer never stumble.

Above, a trio of broad winged hawks circle effortlessly, obliviously, far above the life and death struggle here below. Wherever the hunters are who did not get quite the right shot, I shall reap the benefit of fresh – if a bit scrawny – and wiry meat.

I do not cook the meat until late in the night with the flint and steel I had stored deep in my inner pockets. A loud scream echoes down from above. I take a hunk of raw meat and toss it out to the bobcat I know will raid me when I sleep here at my campsite, anyway.

Sleep overtakes me with the fullness of my gut and who-alls of Mister Owl. This gets my mind to wondering just who-all is out there in the blackness this black night. Some sound, something mechanical, the sound of iron on iron, a trap being set, perhaps, causes my eyes to open. No iron here.

When I focus finally next morning I'm looking straight into the eyes of the bobcat, looking for more to eat, I suppose. Glad I hid the rest of that meat under a huge log so that wild cat could have no more of my precious meat.

A squirrel scolds from above and the bobcat stares at me as if I am to do something about him – the squirrel I mean, not the bobcat. "Shoo! Pshhhh!" I wave my hands and fumble 'round for my musket. The big cat looks warily at me, turns and saunters off as if insulted and bored.

After getting all packed up I scan the hilltop until my eyes rest on a pair of gray boulders and amid the leaves sits the bobcat statue. All of a sudden a paw swipes at the head, disturbing its rest. I retrieve my meat, pull off a chunk and toss it up.

The cat raises its head as if in acknowledgment. The owner of the paw dives for the food but the first wrestles the other to the ground long before the meat is reached.

Chapter Eighty-Two

The days grow shorter and crystalline. Each morning I rise along with all the other creatures and sounds, grateful for each moment I am the owner of myself, my time. I smell more smoke when getting myself up so that I know I am nearing some kind of place where folks are living, habitations. Thank you, Tom for another word that pops into my think head, a head full of stuff clogging things up like a pipe full of coffee grounds. All the words and many things recalled from days gone from me linger on in my mind. Then a nosy wren extinguishes these thoughts, stirs up the air with his warming chatter.

This journey to the gap in the mountains proved longer than I recalled. The sky is a mix of whites and grays as the wind adds his say that without him about, by Mr. Wind's fickle whim, the air swirling about will stay chilly.

Moving takes my mind off my worries. A body in motion calms the rushing brain, lets the rush be in the legs and limbs, not the head. I draw nearer to my destination but cannot smell the expected smoke. Must be this strong breeze carrying it away. Although as Tom would have said – two sides to everything – the breeze should make the smoke to be smelled even farther away.

Sun breaks through the clouds and I see their place below at the end of the long, narrow field that Tom claimed. Why is that door now flapping open in front? The side door looks to be off its hinges completely. Something white flaps on a clothes line giving me hope. Stump low to the ground jumps up and claims my toe. "Damn."

The shouted word dies quick on the breeze. I scan the area for sign of any witnessing bobcat but I am alone. When I reach Tom's place I am even more alone. The clothesline flaps with an old pair of undergarments surely used for cleaning, so full of holes is it. Other old clothes lie scattered within the house.

I find a mealy apple in the corner of the kitchen and ignore its texture to fill my stomach, raiding the place for moldy bread. I scrape the spoil from any other food scraps I uncover and gobble them up.

"Tom. Tom, where have you gone? Did you do this to spite me?" I shout the words and wait for an answer to miraculously come back my way once more.

A huge, buzzing horsefly or maybe a giant yellow bee drifts into the room. The thing buzzes up to the highest wall planks of the space sounding ready to do its will. Buzzing this way and that, thinking it has the world at its call, but for me seeing the reality and the folly that it cannot leave this place. The only way out for it is if it lucks into an open window before thumping at all the panes in the room.

"Lord, is that how you see me?" I say the words aloud, despite there being not a soul about. "Am I that bee or fly or whatever it may be called tearing up the world it thinks is the world when all it is, is trapped in a small space that isn't even a fraction of the world?"

Four dark brown eggs rest in a crude stick basket in the corner. I think of River. It would have been her job to make sure they were all gathered up. Thinking that she left those for me warms my heart. Makes no sense at all to carry any such thoughts in my head right now.

The buzzing fly has headed off into the cold world to find a horse to vex. Presently after finding some meager piles of coffee in the corner of a far shelf I boil the water and sit drinking that while a hornet thinks my rusty tin cup is full of raw beef I suppose.

"Hey you there, what you doing in our house?" A large woman bursts from out of the grove beside the house, a mostly toothless, but younger man trails her.

"This is my friend's house," I offer.

"I don't see any friends about do you, Davey?"

"No. I don't reckon that I do at that, Becky." A dog runs up from just behind him and startles itself with a glance at me. "She won't hurt you, really she won't. Always growls when first getting to know someone."

I sit back down on the step and sip my coffee, eying the two of them. There's not a thing I can do to restore my solitude here. They start to pull things from a pair of burlap sacks leaning up against the side of the house. So dreary were these sacks that I did not notice the things until they started rifling through them.

All of a sudden the man finds something he's been looking for the whole time he rummaged. He sticks the jaw's harp in his mouth, holding it in place with the three prominent teeth he has left and starts in to playing.

"Yankee Doodle keep it up! Yankee Doodle Dandy. Mind the music and your step – "

"And with the gals be handy!" He breaks in on her singing, squints a broad smile directly at me.

The twang of the mouth harp drones on as she hops from one foot to the next. Something about them brings a smile to my face, at the same time I wish I could be a lynx or bobcat up on the hillside just watching these two sillies without being seen, and at once get a pang of homesickness. Home? Ha! Home ain't a place where you be forced to stay, Jamie. I nearly say the words out loud. No. I think I'm just homesick for Gray is all. Only that damned dog growling at me wouldn't take to Gray. The best would kill him just as soon as look at him.

Chapter Eighty-Three

I wasn't exactly going to let them just take over Tom's old place here. Guess River ain't able to get away from Tom and his family, not that she couldn't do such as that.

But now as they snore loudly on the other side of the room which they acted like they owned from the start, I feel something new – damned flea bites right at my elbow, forearm, waist, and ankles. Their devil dog has infested the place just in the short time that they've been here.

"Grrrrrrrr!" The dog growls as soon as I shift my body to leave the room.

"Ra Ra Ra Ra!"

"Bessie, hush!"

Bessie. Sounds like they named their dog for a cow. "I'm going out on the grass to sleep. Thing's full of fleas."

"Oh, all right...." Her words melt into snores matching his, like two blue jays screaming to each other till you cannot even tell if it be one bird or two.

Chapter Eighty-Four

I watch the two of them over the next few days and then the weeks. "Do you want to help me get the rest of those sweet potatoes out of the field there? Still quite a few to get before the frost ruins them for eating."

"Maybe later," they both answer at once it seems.

"I be learning a new song," pipes in Davey.

"And Jamie looks like he's ready to shove that jaw harp down your throat, Davey."

"Now Becky, I can tell when a man likes my music."

I stop in mid-stride and turn to look at the two of them sitting in Tom's porch rockers. I want to say how rarely – no – how I have never heard someone refer to me as a man. It has always been either 'Jamie' or 'slave'. Somehow the flea bites, the laziness, the annoyance of these two clearly living off the hard work of others melts as quick as the cicada screams will come October.

The next day I come back with some fat rabbits I trapped for the pot, enough meat that I don't mind their digging into my efforts and work too.

"You need to help us, Jamie." Davey says the

words calmly.

"Help you?"

Davey lifts a cloth from off Becca's forehead. "She fell over there and hit her head on a rock. Can you stitch her up?"

Becca does not move while I do my crude best with some rabbit gut thread. I tie a clean linen cloth from inside the house over my handiwork on her forehead. Later, while lying out beneath the moon as I have been for some weeks now, Becca stumbles over me.

"He's not what you think he is."

In the gauzy moonlight I see her eye is swollen and dark around the lower edge. "What's she saying about me?" Davey shouts after her.

"I ain't saying nothing."

"Found out she's got another man – she's gone haggard on me like the falconer's hawks what go wild on them from time to – "

"Hog shit. You're a liar, Davey, or whatever your damned name is."

I sit cross-legged on the grass and start to doze as they drift closer to each other. Then their anger melts as they draw together, until their chatter becomes the low annoying sound of a flock of roosting blackbirds in the upper branches of an oak tree.

Chapter Eighty-Five

A jay wakes me up with his warning cry despite it being morning already. The door to the house swings askance on what is left of its hinges. They are gone.

"Grrrrrrr!"

Well, all except for their damned dog.

"Boom! Crack! Pow!" Musket fire chases the dog off. I squint into the sun at the direction of the sound.

"I thought you'd come back, Jamie."

I go to hug Tom. He stiffens at my touch. "What's all that, and whose dog is this?"

"Long story. Can we get some coffee and eat something?" I ask.

"Not much left inside but some sweet potatoes and sour apples."

I move for the front doorway, but notice something moving over where the trees thicken into a glade. A boy tumbles out from the bushes, and I hear someone scold. Then an arm – no two arms – reach out and lift the boy up and back into the concealing bushes.

"What was that about getting something to eat?" Tom read my mind.

I start a fire in the little hearth and put on a pot for coffee. I brush what I can from out of the shelves to darken the hot liquid and take what food that hasn't spoiled to make a sort of stew in the other pot. A thimbleful of stale spices linger in a tiny white sack in the far corner of the kitchen, on a shelf that the recently departed squatters missed. "I saw them down below, Tom."

"Saw who?"

"Shouldn't it be 'whom'?"

"Shut up, Jamie. I don't think about that stuff anymore. We ain't children."

No, Tom, I'm not a child. But in the eyes of the law

I am still a missing piece of property.

"I told you not to – "

"They smelled something real good cooking." Jemima peers into the space that used to be hers and hers alone. A half smile lights up her face. The children rush in and surround her while I offer them apples.

"I don't want that sour old thing."

"Mind your manners, son."

Tom's boy takes a bite and screws up his face. His sister chews hers and smiles. "I like them sour."

"Tart is a better word."

Tom's answer makes a lie of his earlier remarks. I try not to look in her direction. But before I even see her face – gaze on those eyes I know see right through me – I feel the warmth of her smile.

"Does Jamie like River?" asks Tom's girl.

Tom looks up at his wife for some reason, as if searching her face for a way to answer his daughter's bold question.

"Why don't we ask the person you seem to want to gossip about?" Jemima asks. "After all, he is standing right here."

"For now, why don't we see if this stew he started tastes as good as it smells." River's request takes everyone's mind away from the question like a killi bird or killdeer, as Tom calls it, acting over-dramatically, with a fake broken wing to divert an intruder from her babies. She sips with a wooden ladle the wayward mixture, puckering up her lips. "Do we have an onion anywhere? How about a bit more salt if you please, maybe over in the corner of that shelf?"

Chapter Eighty-Six

Later I want to squeeze her just to show her how much that exchange in the kitchen meant to me. The children take turns skipping an old rope before finding the frame of a wagon wheel to race up and down the low hills.

River drifts from the children, from fetching buckets of water, cleaning out the mess in the shed, over to me as I split wood at a huge chestnut stump behind the shed. "He's never said that you couldn't come stay with us, live here like you told me that time awhile back."

I lift my fingers to her lips to stop her from speaking for a time. Then I take her hand and look all about us for a moment. Everyone is busy with their work. The children have found an old chestnut tree that's fallen over recently, and climb the limbs. A closer look lets us see that one of the children has tied a cloth over the eyes of the other. "That's even better. No one will see us go off."

"Go off, James? What did you have in mind?"

"I didn't have anything in mind. Why would you think such as that, River?" One more line, I only need to come up with one more line to make things seem complete, to finish out this exchange. I think. "Good sign. Even that sparrow goes on like he's got not a care in the world, as if we do not exist. Were Gray here he would make poor Mr. Sparrow pay for such an attitude. Poor old cat must be close to ten year old now." A squirrel squeals its strangled cry giving lie to my thoughts that none have noted our presence.

We sit for a handful of precious moments on the mossy bank where leaves and pine needles give the whole place a sweeter smell than out in the heat of the bright sunshine. No need for much talk.

"I've missed that." She breaks the silence at last, surprising me.

"Missed what?"

"Those hands of yours, so solid, yet soft, warming – protecting. They let the world beyond them dissolve." Her warm brown eyes close for a long time. "These hands now work no nails or metal, hands not owned by anyone but you. And me." The words escape in a conspiratorial whisper.

Moss and lichen-encrusted boulders make a nice diversion from the myriad questions spinning through my mind. Queries dog us – well, me at least – just as Gray used to when he was around me. When Gray wanted my complete attention he'd slowly nudge my hand and face with his purring fuzzy head, whiskers caked with dusty old spider webs from some recent exploration.

I step up onto a huge mossy boulder straddling the barely gurgling water of the creek. Folding my arms I dare River to leap up here without my help. She squints over at me defiantly, pulls up her skirt and leaps up as gracefully as a doe. But then she loses her balance and teeters there above the notch formed by a pair of craggy rocks until I grab her.

We sit a long time in silence, holding each other creating treasured moments until she simply rests her head on my shoulder. No thoughts come to our lips. We hold them inside unlike the wrens, crows and jays surrounding us, seemingly never able to keep a secret.

Chapter Eighty-Seven

Later in the day, when we are all back together, and after more of the crazy stew everyone had a hand in adding to, Tom does not argue, nor does Jemima when we go back out to the tall cool grass in the field. Red-pink light lingers to the west of us. I feel hopeful somehow and linked eternally to this person I have been parted from far more than I have been together. The world without is cold and unfeeling. But here is the world for me, one we both agree we shall never be ungrateful for. An owl hoots mournfully and low for a brief time – cold water poured on a fire now warming my body and soul deep to its core. I feel that for River, too.

The dew feels cold on my face as I go to roll onto my back and feel for the warmth somehow missing. The hollow sounds of the blackbirds moving to yet another tree, the tired old jay caws, chickadees, and all of the rest give me a feeling of dread somehow.

The bobcat eyes on me from the bushes. Just hours ago I felt only the warmth of River's brown eyes. Now the cold loneliness of Mr. Bobcat's yellow-green eyes lingering until I force myself to turn from them.

I look once more and see nothing, not even the rustle of a leaf where the furry face just peered my way. No smell of smoke, no laughter of Tom's children. River did not go willingly.

I know River. She would have given me something, a squeeze and kiss or whisper. She knows me, knew waking up and thinking that she would be just a dream would be the only –

"There he is!"

I turn my head as far back around as it will go and see the strange couple again, Davey and Becca – if that is even their true names. They are without their dog. The old story of Judas giving out the whereabouts of Jesus before they murdered him finds its way into my mind.

But now a group of men crowd them out from my sight as the trackers encircle me. I act like a child making something vanish by closing my eyes – as if my not being able to see them also makes me invisible to them as they seize me – I shut my own eyes and suck in the last breath taken in the moments I remain a free man.

Chapter Eighty-Eight

Nothing has happened since I left Monticello. Can that be true? Did I really leave this place for more than two years, living life as my own possession, like every white person does?

The scraping and pushing, constant hammerings enslave my brain more than ever before. Now I cannot escape the sounds. Back then I never really heard the din. Even the sounds of the squirrels, hard at work knocking nuts from off the hickory trees annoy me. I do my best to ignore the shackles now on my ankles.

"Haven't seen Gray in some days." Wilson says pulling open the shed door.

"Gray?"

"Haven't forgotten about your own cat, have you?"

A strangeness lingers in Wilson's eyes, like a stink

bug daring me to remove it from my bed without sharing his nasty smell with me. I can tell he has information he'd rather not tell me. So he talks about Gray instead.

"Figured an owl got him months ago," I offer.

"No, Jamie. Some of the little girls up by the house took to feeding and pampering him. They tied a blue silk ribbon around his neck and he got fat for a time – "

"Gray? Scrawny old Gray, fat?" I fight back the friendliness breaking through in my voice like sun bursting through blue-gray clouds. "But what are the leg irons for? Surprised they – you've waited –"

"There is something I need to tell you."

I stare up into his face for the answer. Wilson raises his hand as if the pressing any further with questions will stop anymore talk completely.

"I will try to be back soon, Jamie."

The dread I felt at awakening alone, without River by my side, returns, only now I fear not the things Wilson has said, but what he has left unspoken. Gray is gone. This is not my place anymore – not that it ever truly was.

Chapter Eighty-Nine

"Hey! Just who I've been wondering about." Ben, one of the newer nail boys from years back looks down at my ankles and takes a deep breath. His full wheelbarrow shows me he's moved on from the nail shed. I don't ask about his current work. "Sorry about old Gray."

"What do you mean?"

"They haven't told you? Just before you were back, not two days ago, a cart and horse got him – just at the bend there where he always liked to play. He was doing real well. Got weight on him for a change."

"And the girls put a blue ribbon with a bell on it to warn the birds of his being around."

"Horses and carts need bells on them to warn of their comings and goings," adds Ben.

"Why won't they let me see Massa Jeff?"

Ben shrugs his broad shoulders. His eyes tell me that he knows otherwise. "Don't feel bad that you ain't to see him. When he's made up his mind, he's made it up."

"And what would that mind be decided on?"

"He's giving you to Lilly. Lilly's only ever sworn if he saw you again he'd sell you on south."

A ragged old shaggy black cat ambles across the road where Gray died. This place belongs to him as much as anyone – no less than it belongs to me. Because I am three-fifths of a man – as Tom once explained – I can own zero fifths of anything, even what I've worked hard at for years and years. The contracts that the whites deal in are written on paper, the same color as them – with ink the color of our skin. But black person cannot have a contract matching their color. That is simply not possible. There is no such thing as white ink.

The squirrels chatter and scratch outside my tiny window, insulted by the existence of anything that they cannot scratch or gnaw through. My things are packed neatly and go with me wherever that may be, with whoever might be taking me away. I looked through them and see they are nice things. Nice clothes bring higher prices.

The breeze awakens me later. The tension of waiting forms a boil on my finger needing to be pierced to relieve the pressure. I take a long, deep breath.

When I open my eyes, I feel a presence beside me. I go to speak. He puts a finger to his mouth in a sign to silence me. The man shakes his head. I see from the cock of the head who it is and feel the lock of the ankle brace go slack and open with a quick snap. Papers are shoved deep into my pocket.

Wilson then grabs my hand and then my forearm. Crows squawk out from the gloom, trying to wake themselves up. I think of Gray and my never seeing him again. My fourth chance. Gray used up his nine chances.

I want to tell Wilson thank you, but know that any sounds whatsoever will end this new freedom. I think back, way back to young Tom's echo of his pa's words. Nothing can stop the man with the right mental attitude from achieving his goal. And I shall now add, that the same words apply to what a woman can do regarding her own goals too.

My mind no longer does the mental fixing of the meaning, the revised explanation that, by man, Mister Thomas Jefferson did not mean to include us slaves. Well, I am a man. I can reply. I pick a rusty nail rod up from off the ground and write words in in the dirt. Thank you.

The End

A Wolf by the Ears

This is Peter Hildebrandt's second novel. As with his first book, it is loosely based on historical events of the time. Hildebrandt lives in Rock Hill, South Carolina in a house some 112 years old.

Made in the USA
Columbia, SC
19 February 2022